THE SILENT WITNESS

Despite her boyfriend's warnings, Sara picks up a hitch-hiker while driving alone through France looking for the grave of her grandfather killed in the war. This encounter leads her to the awesome Chateau du Bois and its dark brooding owner, Jules Clare, whose presence both unnerves and attracts her. He shares the castle with his strange housekeeper and her lumbering son. But, where is Jules' wife?

THE SILENT WITNESS

The Silent Witness

by
June Sutton

178901

DALES LARGE PRINT
Long Preston, North Yorkshire,
England.

British Library Cataloguing in Publication Data

Sutton, June
  The silent witness.
  I. Title
  823.914 [F]
  ISBN 1–85389–197–5
  ISBN 1–85389–224–6 (Pbk)

First Published in Great Britain by Robert Hale Ltd, 1986.

Published in Large Print 1990 by arrangement with Robert Hale
Ltd, London.

Printed and bound in Great Britain by
Redwood Press Limited, Melksham, Wiltshire.

Chapter One

CALAIS was packed with tourists. Sara's nut-brown eyes searched for the right road to take. She could still hear Matthew's words ringing in her ears. 'You must be mad, driving through France on your own. And that old car is never going to make it.'

'Oh, yes, it is,' she muttered now through gritted teeth. 'And so am I!'

She glanced in the driving mirror. There was a row of cars behind her urging her on. Sleek monsters compared to her little car. Some impatient driver sounded his horn.

She ordered herself to stay cool. After all, she had done all her homework before setting out and knew the route almost by heart; she also had an excellent map with her – and all the items one was supposed to have like spare bulbs, beam deflectors . . . everything.

Sara did not want to start her journey on the motorway. It had nothing to do with having to pay tolls, although at this stage she was not really sure how much money

7

she would need to get her to Burgundy and back, but she thought it would be interesting to see more towns on the way. Who knew when she would be coming again? It had taken her long enough to make this first visit.

She admitted to herself it would have been helpful to have had another pair of eyes in the car – perhaps she should have waited until Matthew could have come, too? But that was only a fleeting thought, and soon passed.

After she crossed over the canal and was on the road to Boulogne, she realised she was holding the steering wheel with clenched fingers. She slackened off and relaxed against the seat.

'Paris – here I come!'

Paris was like a magnet to her. City of great painters, great lovers. On her way back she intended to stay in Paris for as long as her money lasted out, and she could not resist staying there for bed and breakfast on her way south.

Soon she was reminded of the real reason she had chosen to come to France, when she drove through Abbeville. Its town centre had been razed to the ground in World War Two. Families there would have lost loved

8

ones, just as she had lost her grandfather.

Sara was tired when she reached Paris. Driving for the first time on the Continent had been more of a strain than she imagined. After finding a parking place at last, she started to look for a room. Immediately she saw how silly she had been not to book ahead.

Matthew had tried to persuade her but, as usual, she had been obstinate. She wondered afterwards if it was because she did not want him organising her life.

'I want to be free to stay where I like when I like,' she had insisted.

'But we are full, Mademoiselle,' wailed the proprietor of the fifth hotel she tried. 'July is the time of all the tourists.'

'Serves me right,' she told herself, then she came upon a cancellation. She considered herself lucky until she saw the poky room in a grimy basement. She lifted the net curtains gingerly and gazed out to a courtyard above her window. She was surrounded by tall, grey buildings and a hundred windows pressed into the walls were staring down at her. It had also started to drizzle.

'Beautiful Paris,' she murmured mournfully.

Later that evening, she sat alone in a bistro sipping coffee. It seemed all wrong to be sitting alone in Paris.

The following morning the car would not start. It coughed and spluttered then died. Sara frowned and tried again, this time pumping the accelerator with her foot. At last, the car sprang into life. She breathed a great sigh of relief and took the ring road round Paris towards the Porte d'Orleans. Suddenly, she saw groups of people waving signs showing their destinations.

'Whatever you do, I'd advise you not to pick up hitch-hikers, Sara,' Matthew had said. 'It isn't wise for a woman on her own. Don't know what you might let yourself in for.'

She drove past the hitch-hikers. It was only after she had left them far behind that she felt extremely mean. Most of them had looked like students – and she had been a student herself once – and had been given lifts. It all seemed a lifetime away and yet she was only twenty-seven now.

It was not long before she was driving through Burgundy. Despite the rain, it looked enchanting. A lovely green and pleasant place to live.

Burgundy was a land of plenty, she had

read, full of stories of dukes and great buildings. A smiling land with mellow wine. The River Yonne was crowded with barges and boats.

Thirteen kilometres after turning off the main road into country lanes, Sara saw a lone figure trudging through the rain wearing orange waterproofs and carrying a huge, blue rucksack. She had no idea if it was a man or woman because the hiker wore an all-enveloping hood. He or she began to wave frantically and Sara could see a Union Jack badge on the rucksack. She stopped the car and wound down the window.

'I'm only going as far as Laffeine but if you—'

'That's great! So am I!' An open, friendly face beamed gratitude at her. 'I'm Steve Grady – a student from London.'

She liked the look of him. 'Sara Parish from Birmingham. Put your rucksack in the back.'

He took off his wet outer garments and she saw a tall, rangy figure with fair shoulder-length hair. She told herself wryly that Matthew would not like this one little bit. But Steve was a pleasant companion and she was glad of someone to talk to at last.

'You don't look like a teacher,' he said, after they had swapped some personal details. 'More like a model.'

She smiled to herself. In no way could she imagine any photographer taking on a model with her wild, red hair. And it would take more than the moisturiser she usually wore, to disguise the freckles on her nose. But she knew she had a good skin and a reasonable figure.

Steve directed her towards Laffeine without having to look at the map.

'You seem to know this area pretty well,' Sara remarked.

'Well, it's more like a second home to me. I've been coming here every year since my Aunt Helen married a Frenchman. One of the useful spin-offs you might say. But what about you? Why have you come to Burgundy? – apart from it being the best place on earth if you love good food and wine.'

She hesitated. 'I . . . I needed a holiday – that's all.'

'Not much happens at Laffeine. Nothing much to do.'

'Oh, there will be for me. You see my grandfather is buried there and this is a sort of pilgrimage for me,' Sara explained quietly.

He looked at her curiously.

'He fought over here in the war,' she continued, sensing his interest. 'He was killed escaping from the Gestapo. Oh – my parents told me so many tales about him.'

'He's quite a hero to you, isn't he?'

'Yes, he is. I used to think about his grave, untended and unvisited in some quiet country churchyard and I made up my mind that one day I would visit it.'

'Did your parents ever come?'

'They intended to, but somehow never managed it. My father died several years ago and my mother . . . my mother very recently.' It was still painful to think about her. A deep overwhelming sadness filled her heart. Sara blinked away the threatening tears.

'So you're alone now?' Steve said quietly.

'Oh, no.' She swallowed and tried to steady her voice. 'There's Matthew, he teaches at the same school. I've known him for many years and we're getting married when I get back.'

'Why isn't he here with you?' Steve asked, glancing at her quickly.

'He's taking a school group camping in Wales. Anyway, he isn't very keen on travelling abroad,' Sara added.

'Smokes a pipe and likes gardening, does he?' Steve asked, with the merest hint of amusement in his voice.

Sara decided the conversation had gone far enough – it was becoming too personal. She had already told him more than she intended.

Her thoughts strayed back to her mother. She remembered wondering if she was going mad after her mother had died. How she had continued to lay the table for two – and planned meals for both of them. The years of looking after her had become a habit she could not break.

The family doctor had said it was nothing to worry about – but it would be a good idea for Sara to get right away from the house. Have a holiday.

'Do something you have always wanted to do,' he had advised. 'Just for yourself. Leave Matthew here. He'll be waiting when you get back.'

Chapter Two

THE road became more winding and the car seemed to be labouring as it pulled up the hills.

'What time is your aunt expecting you?' Sara asked.

She noticed the change in Steve's tone at once. He no longer sounded jocular.

'My aunt is not there at the moment. She hasn't been for some time. Jules, her husband, insisted that I didn't change our usual arrangements and as I haven't anywhere else to go – my parents are dead, too – the lure of this place was still as great as ever.' He was silent for a moment before adding coldly, 'Dear old Uncle Jules,' he said.

They were almost at Laffeine when Steve spoke again. 'You drive very well,' he said sincerely.

Sara was pleased by his remark. Matthew had always given the impression he thought a woman's place was in the passenger seat.

'I like to think I've adapted quickly to driving on the right,' she told him smiling. 'But it startles me when drivers shoot out of side roads in front of me.'

'You must watch out for signs saying

"Priorité à droite." '

His French was fluent, and Sara made a mental resolution there and then to improve her own. At the moment, she felt she sounded like a bumbling schoolgirl.

She looked at him quickly. 'Which way now? The road forks ahead.'

'Left. You'll come to a steep hill in a moment.'

The car managed the hill all right, but Sara found she couldn't engage third gear. 'Oh, no! It's stuck in second.' They coasted down the hill then stopped.

'Something tells me you've got trouble.' Steve said, as they sat gazing at the road ahead.

'I know,' she answered irritably. 'I may have stripped a gear.'

Steve hopped out. 'Well, we'll just have to walk the rest of the way,' he told her cheerfully.

Sara did not think the situation called for frivolity, but when he lifted the car boot lid she was forced into an embarrassed grin.

He whistled. 'You're certainly prepared for emergencies,' he said, looking at all the spare parts. 'I don't know anything about car engines,' he added apologetically.

'Is it far to walk into Laffeine?' Sara

16

asked then, dragging her case out of the car. 'And what's more important, is there a garage?'

'You're almost in Laffeine. Round the next corner you'll see some cottages with paint peeling – just like Jules' place. That's the start. Yes, there is a garage. Come on – I'll show you.'

No one at the garage spoke English, and she was glad Steve was there to translate for her.

He turned to her. 'It doesn't sound too good, I'm afraid. They are going to bring the car in to look at it, but say it sounds as if it needs replacement parts.'

Sara groaned to herself. 'I wonder if you would please ask them if they know of a small hotel round here?'

'There's no need for that,' he replied with a smile. 'You can come and stay at Jules' place.'

She looked at him in surprise. 'I couldn't possibly impose—'

'You wouldn't be! All my friends doss down there when they come to France.' From the way he spoke, Sara assumed his uncle had a guest house.

'I'd be delighted then,' she said. 'Thank you, Steve.'

'You won't see much of him. He shuts himself away writing suspense fiction most of the time . . . I sometimes wonder where he digs up all his macabre ideas for stories.'

Again, she thought she heard a touch of rancour in his voice.

The rain had stopped and the sun was breaking through the clouds.

Steve informed her they would take the short-cut through the woods to his uncle's house. There was a fresh, tangy smell of warm earth, and she found it refreshing to be in the open air once more.

After they had been walking for a while, she saw a wide, silver lake through a clearing in the trees. It was fringed by weeping willows and reeds, with water-lilies floating on the surface.

'Oh, isn't it pretty!' she exclaimed.

'We go boating in there sometimes, but you have to be careful,' Steve told her. 'It's deep, and choked with weeds. Even a strong swimmer could get into difficulties in there.'

Sara found she had to put her case down several times and rest.

Steve was able to stride ahead, leading the way with his huge rucksack on his back. She had refused to hand the case over and give him even more weight to carry.

She saw him waiting for her at the far end of an avenue of trees. When she reached him, she caught her breath and stared!

Rising from a high, flat mound, like something out of a fairy story, was an enormous, stone building with a massive round tower at each corner.

'Welcome to Château du Bois,' Steve said with a casual wave of his hand.

Her eyes dilated. 'Who – who lives there?'

'Uncle Jules.'

'It's converted then? Into a hotel?' she asked faintly.

'No – it's the family seat.'

With a certain amount of trepidation, Sara followed him up to the terraces. It was a very grand place – but there was nothing tidy about the gardens surrounding it. There were plenty of overgrown shrubberies and weed-filled lawns. Here surely was an owner who believed in giving Nature her way. Someone who didn't give a jot for outward show.

As they reached the central courtyard she recalled Steve's earlier remark. The plain, grey walls had mortar falling from them. She wondered if the inside was as rundown.

Steve yanked the bell-pull and she heard a

clanging far inside the château.

'When was this place built?' she asked.

'There's no need to whisper,' he answered with a laugh. 'I think it was originally fifteenth century, but there's been lots done to it since, of course.'

The great door was opened then by a fresh-faced girl in a flowered dress. 'Monsieur Steve!' she exclaimed delightedly.

'Hello, Jacqueline.'

''Ello!' the girl echoed, giggling.

As they followed her, Steve told Sara that Jacqueline was one of the maids. 'Her English is non-existent, so you'll have to brush up on your French.'

Sara saw at once that the exterior of the château had been no indication of the splendour to be found inside. They went into a wide hall with tapestries on the walls and a high, ornate ceiling.

'I think Jules may be away,' Steve said, then, breaking into her admiring thoughts. 'I'll go and find someone. Take a seat.'

She ignored the crimson-padded chair he pointed to, and walked slowly round the grand hall. She was feeling more and more apprehensive.

Did Steve really have the authority to invite her to someone else's home? She was a little overwhelmed by her surroundings and not entirely at ease with the situation.

Chapter Three

SUDDENLY the almost holy silence was shattered by a high-pitched piercing yell. A small boy about three or four with corn-coloured hair came hurtling towards her. She dodged to one side and he slid to a standstill and stared. Despite his dirty face, he was an attractive-looking child.

'Michael!' Steve came racing after him. The boy turned away from Sara and ran screaming across the hall again. He dissolved into giggles when Steve caught him and hoisted him on to his shoulders.

'Come and meet my friend, Sara,' Steve said. 'Sara, this pest is my cousin Michael – Jules' and Helen's son.' He lifted Michael down to the floor and stood holding his shoulders.

Michael held out his hand. '*Bonjour*, Mademoiselle.'

'*Bonjour*, Michael.' She racked her brains for her schoolgirl French. '*Comment allez-*

vous?'

'Don't let him fool you, Sara – he speaks English as well as I do,' Steve informed her with a grin.

'Better!' Michael retorted. He wore scruffy dungarees over a blue and white striped T-shirt.

Sara approved of children being allowed to stretch themselves mentally and physically but her experienced eyes told her Michael was under stress. It was something about the enormous, bright-blue eyes, their expression alternating between devilment and sad dreaminess.

'Nanny wants you,' Steve said to the child.

'No!'

'Oh, good, you've got him!' a pleasant Scottish voice exclaimed, and Sara saw a middle-aged woman hurrying towards them. 'Come along, Michael – no more tantrums; there's a good boy.' She bent to take Michael's hand and he slipped away from Steve and charged towards one of the doors. The woman glanced up to smile apologetically at Sara then she gave chase.

'That,' Steve said ruefully, 'is poor, over-worked Miss Betts, Michael's nanny.'

'He looks quite a handful,' Sara

remarked.

'Hardly surprising,' Steve murmured.

Sara was about to ask him what he meant when she saw a strange figure walking across the hall.

The woman made no sound as she glided towards them in soft-soled shoes. Sara found it impossible to guess how old she was – late sixties – or more, and there was a grace and dignity in her bearing which Sara was to notice later in many mature Burgundian women.

Her shiny brown hair was peppered with grey and drawn into a bun at the nape of her neck, emphasising her strong facial features and deep forehead. Although her figure was on the plump side it was nevertheless attractively curvaceous.

She smiled at Steve. 'Monsieur Steven! It is good to see you again. Now we know summer has really come, *n'est-ce pas?*'

'How are you, Madame?' Steve asked politely. 'Sara, this is Madame Darle Brigidet without whom Château du Bois would cease to function altogether.'

The housekeeper laughed, and the skin round her grey eyes crinkled.

'Madame Darle,' Steve continued in his disarming manner, 'this is my friend who would like to stay with us for a while until her car is repaired – Miss Sara Parish.'

At the sound of her name, it seemed to Sara that the woman's expression changed. She looked strangely perplexed for a moment – as if she were trying to remember something. But almost immediately the look vanished and she clapped her hands together.

'But, of course. There are always rooms ready. Please follow me, Mademoiselle. You shall have the best – *oui*?'

She led the way up a winding, stone staircase and along some dimly-lit passages where time seemed to have stood still. Suddenly, Madame Darle stopped and peered ahead of her.

'Pascal?' she called quietly.

Sara started.

A man appeared from out of the shadows. He had a heavy, lumbering appearance. As he came closer she guessed that he was in his forties and dressed in a navy vest with muscles in his arms like a weight-lifter. His trousers were held up by a wide, black leather belt with a huge, brass buckle.

Madame Darle spoke urgently to him in French, almost as if she was reprimanding him.

He shrugged and gestured with his hands, then he glanced curiously at Sara. Although he was going bald in the centre of his head, she saw that his eyebrows were thick and joined in a bushy mass, giving him a strangely primitive appearance. She watched Madame Darle pat him affectionately on the cheek.

'This is my son, Pascal,' she said to Sara. 'He is – what you call? Handyman and gardener. He will carry your case.'

As Madame Darle carried on walking, Pascal gave Sara a sidelong look that seemed to strip the clothes from her body.

She gave a little shiver and hurried after the housekeeper.

Sara found her room enchanting. It was a mixture of the old and new, obviously furnished with the visitor's comfort in mind. There was a heavily-beamed ceiling and a canopied, stone fireplace while tall windows allowed the Burgundy sunshine to stream in across the thick-pile carpet and pretty, flowered duvet on the four-poster.

'If you ring the bell when you are ready to come down, Mademoiselle,' Madame Darle said pleasantly, 'the maid will show you the way.'

Pascal placed her case by the bed, nodded

respectfully, and went out.

Had she been mistaken about him? Sara wondered. There, in the bright, spacious room he didn't seem a bit sinister, only very helpful. Long, dark passages could play havoc with the mind, she decided.

Left alone, she wandered about the room enjoying the sensation of luxury around her. Then she slipped out of her clothes and went into the bathroom to soak in the big, square bath. Flame-haired, she stood drying herself in the rays of the sun, feeling relaxed and refreshed.

After she had dressed in a light skirt and blouse, she decided to try to find her own way downstairs again instead of bothering anyone. Halfway along the narrow corridor she stopped abruptly and listened hard. She could hear a woman crying. Then, to her horror, there was the distinct sound of a slap. Then a deep, hoarse whisper.

Her heart quickened when she heard a noise behind her.

'Mademoiselle?' a voice said.

Sara smiled in relief. The maid, Jacqueline, nodded, indicating she would show Sara the way down. She did not appear to have noticed the sobbing or, if she had, thought nothing of it.

Sara wondered what it was that made her feel suddenly nervous.

Chapter Four

SUPPER that evening was a gastronomic delight to Sara, who was ravenously hungry. There was only herself and Steve at the long table in the dining-room. Michael was safely in Miss Betts' care while Jules apparently was in Paris, visiting his publisher.

For starters there was onion soup with croutons and grated cheese and this was followed by peppered steak, together with a full-bodied Beaujolais.

'You enjoy – *oui*?' Madame Darle asked.

'Most definitely, yes,' Steve enthused. 'But then, I do always enjoy food here. And after I've downed this lot I shall lie on the terrace in the last of the sunshine and let it all digest very, very slowly. What about you, Sara?'

She laughed. 'If I can move, I think I would like to walk to the village.'

'Such energy! You are going to have bags of time for seeing the village. I have a feeling that car of yours is going to be off the road for quite a while.'

'Well, I'm not too sorry about that. This is such a lovely place, it would be a pity not to stay for a while.'

'Well, you know you can stay here as long—'

'Oh, no. I didn't mean . . . I couldn't impose on your uncle's hospitality for too long. If the repairs are going to take any length of time, I shall look for a small hotel. It will give me a marvellous opportunity to explore Laffeine and find out if anyone remembers my grandfather. Perhaps I'll find out who he stayed with and who his friends were. I want to know all that happened to him here. And I'll take some photos, of course.'

'Of your grandfather's grave? Did you know Sara's grandfather is buried in Laffeine, Madame Darle?' Steve asked, looking at her.

'Is he?' the housekeeper was ladling fresh fruit salad into small bowls.

Jacqueline came into the room carrying a cut-glass bowl full of home-made ice-cream, and handed it to her.

Steve turned back to Sara. 'Your stay here will allow you to meet some of the older folk in the village and get to know the full story of what happened to your grand-father. Come to think of it, Madame Darle, you must have been here when he was killed by the Gestapo.'

'Yes, Madame,' Sara added eagerly. 'His name was Parish, like mine, Sergeant John Parish.'

The bowl of ice-cream dropped like a stone from the housekeeper's hands. It crashed into tiny pieces. She stood like a statue, fists clenched, her skin suddenly white.

Sara and Steve jumped up immediately to help.

Madame Darle, however, sprang to life again and spoke in French to the maid, who ran to fetch a dustpan and brush.

'I am so sorry!' she said apologetically. 'But the dish was very cold, I will get more of the ice cream . . .'

Before they could reply, she had gone.

'Well, I'm damned!' Steve exclaimed. 'I've never seen her do anything careless like that before. She must be feeling her age, but then she's the type who will carry on until she drops. Worships the ground old Jules walks on. Won't leave until he chucks her out, and he isn't likely to do that.'

'You know, Steve, she looked – almost frightened just now,' Sara said thoughtfully.

'So would you if you'd dropped that bowl. It was probably priceless.'

Sara still felt uneasy. There was a strange atmosphere in the château, something she couldn't define.

'Steve – where is your aunt?' she asked tentatively.

'I told you, she isn't here,' he replied woodenly. 'Oh, I suppose you might as well know,' he continued. 'She left Jules last year and nobody has heard from her since.'

'And Michael as well?' Sara asked, wide-eyed. 'She left him?'

'According to the gossips she trotted off with her lover.' Suddenly, he threw down his napkin. 'I don't want any more. I'm going outside,' he said abruptly.

Sara was sorry she had brought up the subject, but by the time she was ready to go into the village, Steve's good humour had returned.

'Don't go through the wood at this time of night,' he called, as he lay on the sun-lounger. He waggled his fingers in mock horror. 'You don't know what you might see . . . nasty, slithery snakes . . .'

'Are there snakes in that wood?'

30

'Oh, there's the odd adder waiting to—'

'Rubbish,' she answered, laughing.

'And remember every village has its local idiot waiting to pounce on pretty, young maidens as they tiptoe through the bracken.'

'I'm neither pretty nor young,' she retorted and left, swinging her camera and the map he had lent her of the district.

Chapter Five

SARA took the small, country lane that led from the château to Laffeine. She had no intention of taking the short cut through the wood on her own. The evening was warm and pleasant and the path overlooked fresh, green fields with cattle peacefully grazing.

When she reached the village there was not a soul to be seen. She told herself the French obviously believed in stretching out their evening meal. Old houses, tumbled down narrow roads, an air of decay about them – but if the château was anything to go by it would be no indication of what they were like inside. The only sound she could hear was the clack of her own heels on the cobbles.

Suddenly, a shutter clattered. She jumped. She could have sworn a face peered through the curtains but, of course, it would be normal for the villagers to be curious about a stranger.

The ancient church fitted its surroundings perfectly. Sara wondered if she should find the priest and ask his permission to look round the churchyard. But the place was deserted and she wanted to take photos before the sun went down. Anyway, it was not like exploring inside a church, she reasoned.

The little churchyard was surrounded by a low, stone wall. It would not be difficult to find the grave. But it all felt so peculiar, so unreal. Almost as if she were looking for a stranger, and yet her parents had told her so much about her grandfather, that Sara had always felt an affinity with him.

They had said she was like him – the man she had only seen in photographs, the man with kind, humorous eyes and a great zest for life.

Then she saw the grave.

It was tucked in a corner, in a sheltered spot, and was beautifully tended with fresh flowers on it. She stared at the headstone, unable to believe that at long last the two of them were meeting.

'Sergeant John Stanway Parish,' she read. There was a tightness in her throat. Then came the strangest moment of all. Without any difficulty she was able to translate the inscription as if she had been speaking French all her life.

'He gave his life so others might live.'

Her eyes smarted. 'Hello, Grandad, I'm Sara and I've come for all of us.'

A dark, drifting shadow slid across the grave as the sun slipped between scudding clouds. Sara watched it, mesmerised. She felt an uncanny closeness to the man buried there. Tomorrow she would return with flowers, but this was the occasion she would never forget.

She glanced up at the sky. If she was quick and chose her moment, she could take some photographs. Her hand moved down towards the camera. Suddenly there was a cracking sound in her ears.

A bullet had missed her arm by inches!

It ricocheted with a hiss off the headstone. She leaped back in terrified amazement. Her mouth turned to dust. No noise came out of it. She began to run. She didn't know where she was running, only that she had to get away. Instinct warned her she was racing for her life.

With sobbing breaths, she found herself on the edge of the wood leading to the château. She plunged between the trees. They had looked so attractive when she had gone that way with Steve, but now formed menacing, dark shapes above her.

The light was failing rapidly. As she ran, she looked for the lake but could see it nowhere, nor the avenue that led directly to the château.

The ground was soggy and dank. Her legs were like lead. There was a pain like barbed wire round her chest. She fell against the trunk of a gnarled oak tree and clung there, gasping. Whoever was following her would surely hear her breathing!

There was a rustle in the undergrowth. She waited, motionless. Waiting for . . . whom? Who would want to kill her? What had she done?

The pain in her ribs began to ease. She forced her brain to work for itself. If she came face to face with someone with a gun there was very little she could do about it, so she had to make sure she stayed behind the would-be murderer. Then there was plenty she could do to try to defend herself.

But it was with great relief she realised the man – or woman – must have lost her. After waiting for what seemed like an eternity, she decided it was safe to go on. She had no idea which path to take. After a moment she started to run again like the wind in what she thought was the direction of the château.

She almost fell into the man's arms.

He was a dark-bearded figure and towered above her. She could see his eyes glinting in the half-darkness. Hands made of iron gripped her.

This time, she screamed louder than she had ever screamed in her life!

Chapter Six

THE man shook her, gripping her shoulders with his strong fingers. He spoke urgently in French.

Sara did not understand – she punched out at him. He caught hold of her wrists and held them in the air. She was helpless and unable to move. Suddenly, she was angrier than she had ever been in her life. She

35

kicked his shin as hard as she could.

'*Mon Dieu!*' he roared and let go with one hand. She lashed out again at the other shin. This time he bent to catch hold of her leg and jerked it. She overbalanced and went sprawling in the dirt. He fell on top of her.

'Help!' she screamed.

He leaned away from her with a look of surprise, but still holding her arms pinned to the ground. 'You are English!' he exclaimed.

'Let me up!' she panted.

'Listen, English tigress,' he told her coldly. 'Listen to me. I do not intend to hurt you. I try to tell you this, but you fight like an animal. Tell me, what are you doing here on private property? I allow no one to charge through my woods, disturbing my game . . .'

'Your woods?' Sara replied chokingly. 'Who are you?'

'I am Jules Clare and this is my land. More to the point – who are you?'

It was unbelievable to Sara that this was Steve's uncle. She had expected an older man. Steve had called him 'Old Jules.' This man looked barely forty. This man – kneeling astride her, his gun at his side.

'Let me up,' she repeated angrily.

36

'If you give me your word not to scream. I told you – I have not the slightest intention of hurting you.'

She was conscious of his weight and the pressure of his thighs against hers. 'You are hurting me now,' she snapped. He swiftly pulled her to her feet, and she wiped the mud off her dress.

She scowled up at him. 'I'm not a trespasser, you know. It so happens I ran through this wood because someone was chasing me. I was frightened.'

'Frightened?' he said. 'You can fight like a man!'

'I was shot at!' she persisted, suddenly feeling very miserable and tired.

He picked up his shotgun. 'I am the only one allowed to shoot in this wood and I can assure you, Mademoiselle, it is not my habit to fire at women.'

Sara was exasperated at his inability to grasp her situation. 'I wasn't shot at in the wood. It was outside the church.'

'The church?' he echoed, with disbelief in his voice.

'Yes!'

Cynicism crept into his words now, spoken deeply and with mocking politeness. 'But, of course! The tiny church at Laffeine

37

is noted as a meeting place for the criminal fraternity in the village.'

Sara sighed and shook her head.

'Mademoiselle,' he continued, 'if you did hear shooting then you may be sure the poachers are up to their old tricks. I assume you are a tourist? May I suggest that in future when you visit a strange town, you obtain a good map of the area first and study it carefully to discover which properties are private and which are open to holiday-makers.

'I would also point out that your little knowledge of the martial arts would not be sufficient to protect you from what many men have first and foremost on their minds. You are very unwise to be wandering alone in a place with which you are not familiar. You understand my meaning?'

'Perfectly,' she said coldly.

'What is your name?'

'Sara Parish,' she said, flicking her hair back from her face.

'And you stay – where?'

She paused. She wanted her reply to stun him into silence. To shame him into apologising to someone who was a guest in his own house, for his curt behaviour. She savoured her moment.

38

'I am staying at the Château du Bois, Monsieur.'

There was silence between them. She could see his eyes glittering in the darkening night.

At last he spoke. There was no apology, only a stony acceptance of the situation. 'I presume my nephew has arrived then, bringing the usual collection of "friends" along with him?'

'Only me,' she intoned. 'And I shall look for a hotel tomorrow.'

He called over his shoulder as he stomped away from her. 'I warn you – the hotel here does not welcome penniless hitch-hikers.'

Sara had decided straight away that she did not like the man who had trampled over her in the same way he thought she had trampled across his wood. But as she saw his tall, straight back disappearing through the trees, a panic seized her. She did not want to be left alone again. Fear overcame dislike and she hurried after him.

'I suppose you know the way from here?' he said when they reached the château. 'If not, I shall have to call one of the maids. My housekeeper is visiting in the village tonight.'

'I know my way, thank you.'

'May I ask where you met my nephew?'

'On the road.'

He grunted. After he had said a brief Good night,' Sara went to find Steve.

'I believe he went to the village just after you,' Miss Betts said when Sara asked if she had seen him. 'Are you all right, dear? You look a wee bit pale.'

'Miss Betts, I went to the cemetery to see my grandfather's grave and someone tried to shoot me!' Sara said, needing someone to believe her.

'Oh, no! Are you sure? This is a very peaceful little place. I can't imagine . . . I would think it was the poachers out again. They do have their fun from time to time. Oh, yes – it was surely the poachers you heard.'

'In a churchyard?'

Mary Betts laughed. 'Anywhere. I've often seen rabbits running over the graves when we go to church.'

Sara did not pursue the subject. It was obvious no one was prepared to believe her. But, apart from the shot that had narrowly missed her, she was sure she had heard someone else besides Jules in the wood.

Just then, she noticed Pascal walking across the hall carrying logs for one of the

40

huge, open fireplaces.

'Has Pascal been here all evening?' she asked on impulse. Immediately, she was ashamed of the suspicions lurking inside her.

Mary Betts glanced at her curiously. 'Why, yes. All evening.'

'Of course,' Sara murmured, acutely embarrassed.

Chapter Seven

THE next morning she woke to see the sun streaming through the windows. As she showered and dressed, she wished she could get rid of the sense of foreboding at the thought of meeting Jules Clare again. He obviously thought she had tagged on to his nephew with hopes of free board and lodgings. And he also believed she was completely scatter-brained.

When she went into breakfast, Steven, Miss Betts, and Michael were already seated at the table.

Michael began to giggle and show off when he saw her and Steve grinned at her.

A maid, who was obviously pregnant, poured her dark, steaming-hot coffee.

Sara quickly decided it was a flavour she would easily come to enjoy.

'How did the walk go?' Steve asked. 'Did you find your grandfather's grave?' He spread thick, yellow butter on his croissant.

'Yes, I did,' Sara replied.

'You'll see Jules this morning, Mary says he came home last night.'

'Quite right,' a deep voice said from the doorway.

Steve rose to his feet. '*Bonjour*, Uncle Jules,' he said in a respectful tone.

'*Bonjour*, how are you, Steven?' Jules walked across and grasped his nephew's hand.

Michael slid down from his chair and hurled himself at his father. 'Pa-pa!'

Jules swung him in the air then kissed him on both cheeks. His eyes met Sara's and she felt herself growing hot.

'Oh – this is my friend, Sara,' Steve said. 'She is—'

'We have met already.' Jules gave a brief nod in her direction. He turned back to his son. 'Come, Michael, finish your breakfast.'

'I don't want it!'

'Eat.'

Michael looked at the table, then at his father, appraising the situation.

Jules shrugged. 'If you want to go out for your walk then you must eat first.'

Michael climbed back on to his seat.

How alike they were, father and son, Sara thought. Both with the same vivid blue eyes, but in Jules' case there was a sensuousness behind the heavy lids that made her uncomfortable without understanding why. He had a straight nose and black beard that started just below his cheekbones. His thick hair was as dark, though she could see one or two white hairs here and there.

He looked up and caught her staring at him and she blushed.

'Thank you, Crystal,' he said to the maid who was pouring his coffee. There was no mistaking the adoration in her eyes as she smiled back. Jules leaned towards Michael. 'If you do go out this morning, you must be on your guard.' He lowered his voice. 'I think there are tigers in the wood.'

Michael threw back his head and laughed loudly. 'I want to see a tiger.'

Sara felt the colour rush to her cheeks again. She could not wait to get away from the table.

'And what are you doing these days, Steve? Passing all your exams?' Jules asked casually. In the silence that followed he continued, 'And what are your holiday plans?'

'Well, I intend to earn some money, of course. I'm not going to sponge off you all the time. Later on I shall go grape-picking—'

'I see,' Jules said, resignation in his voice.

'For now I thought I might do a bit of fishing and shooting – if that's all right?'

'Of course – but take care. By the way – did you go shooting last night?'

Sara's brown eyes slanted quickly in Jules' direction.

'No . . . I would ask first if it was OK . . . Why do you ask?' Steve said.

'A shot only just missed your friend – or so she tells me.'

Steve glanced in surprise at Sara then back to Jules who said dryly, 'Have you known one another long?'

Steve went on to tell him about their meeting and the car breaking down.

'So you teach, do you?' Jules asked, with what she suspected was a note of amusement in his voice. 'And who do you teach?'

'I teach in the infants' department,' she replied in clipped tones, before hurriedly excusing herself from the table.

Later, she was walking across the great hall when Michael came careering towards her in a pedal car. She dodged out of the way and he began to pursue her. At last, she pretended to collapse in a chair.

'Will you come for a walk with us?' he asked.

'I'd like to, Michael, but I have to go to the village.'

'Why?'

'To call at the garage.'

'Why?'

'My car is being repaired. I want to find out how long it's going to take.'

'You can borrow my car.' His eyes were wide and appealing.

Sara bent down to the little boy. 'That is very sweet of you, Michael. Thank you.' At that moment she sensed someone watching them and glanced up to see Jules Clare at the far end of the hall. Then Mary Betts appeared and headed for Michael.

'I'm not coming. I'm not coming!' he yelled and pedalled away from her, giggling.

Chapter Eight

STEVE had decided to go to Laffeine with Sara. 'I want to get out of Jules' way this morning,' he confided. 'He's got that do-gooder look in his eye as if he's going to find me all sorts of interesting and educational things to occupy my time – like helping him with his research or something. Then the conversation will drift to the subject of exams and how I am or am not getting on, and as I'm not, I think I'll give his company a miss for the time being.'

'Look – we've no need to walk,' he added. 'We can use one of the cars.'

'Jules' cars?'

He nodded – and Sara said she would prefer to walk!

She found the atmosphere in Laffeine quite different from the previous evening. People stood about gossiping, while children skipped and played in the narrow streets between old, half-timbered buildings with leaded lights. It reminded her of an old painting.

The news from the garage was optimistic. The car needed spare parts, but could be ready in a few days.

'Not bad for a small place like this,' Steve

said. 'He appears to be quite a good mechanic. Come on, I'll buy you a drink,' he added. 'That's a big bonus about France – no licensing hours.'

'Steve – look, I think I ought to find somewhere else to stay,' Sara said, as she walked beside him in the sunshine.

'What?'

'I can't impose on your family. I had an idea your uncle did bed-and-breakfast, or something, but when I saw—'

'Good God, it would be the height of rudeness to leave now and move somewhere else in the village! Madame Darle would never live it down. The French are very touchy about their hospitality—'

'I haven't noticed your uncle being–' she began, then stopped.

'What's with you two? What's been going on?' Steve demanded. 'There was a very peculiar atmosphere between you both. I was watching you at breakfast. How did you come to meet?'

Sara sighed. 'I simply met him when I was coming back through the wood last night.'

'Oh, no! I told you not to go that way.'

'You only told me to beware of snakes. You didn't say anything about an irate man with a gun.'

'He loathes anyone walking through there. Oh, he's generous enough in other ways – I'll give him that – but, as far as that precious wood is concerned, you'd think he'd got buried treasure stacked away in the place. He's crazy.'

'But you took a short cut—'

'I know which paths to stick to. And I know where he usually goes shooting and where he sits writing. So do the poachers, and, like me, they steer clear of those areas.'

'Steve, I'm sorry. I'm afraid I caused trouble for you. After all, I am your guest.'

'Jules, me, and trouble are old acquaintances. Anyway, to hell with him. This is my aunt's home as well as his, and she wouldn't have bothered about anyone walking through the woods. She was human!'

'Was?'

'Is – was – who knows? I tell you, it was all different when she was at the château. She loved me bringing lots of friends here. God, we had some fantastic times – except Jules had a habit of being the spectre at the feast. I remember when we had a midnight barbecue—'

As he talked, Sara began to feel a strange

48

sneaking sympathy for Jules. Summer after summer he had his privacy invaded and yet he still carried on inviting Steve, even though Steve's aunt was no longer there. And Steve still carried on with his habit of bringing along others.

She could understand Jules standing guard over his last retreat – his beautiful wood. A place where he found peace and quiet. She understood about privacy. Although she had loved her mother dearly, there had been times when she was looking after her when she had longed for it.

'So what are you going to do?' Steve asked, breaking into her thoughts. 'Tell Madame Darle you will be moving into a hotel where you'll be more comfortable than at the château?'

Sara gave a smile. 'No, Steve, I won't be doing that.'

'Good! I shan't be cooped up alone with Jules, after all.'

They were approaching the small square when Steve seized hold of her arm. 'Come on – I'll take you to meet Pierre. He probably knew your grandfather.'

Sara found herself hustled into a little butcher's shop. A small, elderly man wearing a stained overall immediately came across to Steve with his hand outstretched.

'Monsieur Steve!' he exclaimed delightedly.

As usual, Steve was able to converse in French without any difficulty.

Sara stood back shyly.

Two women were serving behind the counter. The older one nodded and smiled in Sara's direction, but the middle-aged one seemed to be avoiding her eyes and continued slicing through pork chops with sharp efficiency.

She had red, muscular arms and broad shoulders that would have done justice to any man. When the older woman had finished serving her customer she hurried over to the elderly man who was beckoning her.

Steve turned to Sara. 'This is Monsieur Pierre Narbon and his wife, Claudette. I have been telling them who you are.'

When Sara put out her hand, Pierre seized it eagerly. She thought he was never going to stop shaking it, and Claudette was as welcoming.

'Mademoiselle Parish,' Pierre said, slowly in English. 'It is wonderful to meet you. We remember the soldier who came here –

your *grandpère* – so long ago – but we remember.'

His wife turned excitedly to the other woman serving and spoke rapidly in French.

'You have caused a furore,' Steve said. 'Madame Narbon is telling their assistant, Louise, about the granddaughter of the brave soldier who was killed here in the war. That at last someone has come to visit his grave.'

Louise, however, did not appear impressed and only nodded to Sara before going on with her work.

Pierre shrugged almost apologetically. 'Louise is too young to remember the war.'

'Many of our young people grow up without knowing of the hardship, the tortures,' Claudette said sadly, pronouncing her words slowly. Then she spoke in French to Steve.

He turned to Sara. 'She says they don't want to glorify war, but it is something that must never be allowed to happen again. Therefore people must not forget.'

'How long did my grandfather stay in the village? I should love to hear anything you can tell me about him,' Sara said to the Narbons.

Claudette smiled and nodded. 'It is best you come for supper and we talk.'

'Thank you, Madame.'

It was not so easy for Sara to leave the shop now. Villagers who had heard she was there began to crowd in, some to stare and others, usually the elderly, to shake her hand vigorously. How kind they all were, she thought, and how welcoming. It was ridiculous to think that any of them might have shot at her. The explanation about the poachers was obviously the right one.

'Madame Gouvan!' Pierre shouted, and drew a tall woman towards Sara.

'Madame Gouvan looks after the soldier's grave with the other women,' he explained.

'Oh, please, Steve – tell her how very grateful my parents would have been and how beautiful the grave looks.'

Steve spoke to the woman who, for a moment, looked uncomfortable.

Sara wondered why.

'She says it is the least she could do,' Steve said, translating seconds later.

Another of the older women began to chatter to Sara. 'That British Tommy – he came to the village one night. Running from the Germans. We put him to hide in – how you say? – top room.'

'Attic?' Sara suggested.

'*Oui* – attic of . . .'

At this moment, Louise directed a torrent

of angry French at Pierre and waved a raw joint of meat above her head.

'I think we are causing a hold-up here, Steve. Perhaps I can take up Madame's offer to talk to her over supper one night?' She looked at Madame Narbon.

'But of course, *ma petite!*' Claudette exclaimed warmly, understanding the situation.

When they left the shop, Sara asked Steve who owned it. She had been surprised by Louise's outburst. The woman had eventually pushed through the small crowd to reach Pierre, jostling Sara as she did so.

Steve grinned. 'Pierre owns it, but Louise has been an assistant there for years – a very good one, too – she is more like one of the family now. Pierre tries not to tangle with her. Would you? Look at the size of her!'

'I shouldn't have stayed in there so long.'

'Pierre and his wife didn't mind at all. Far from it.'

'Steve,' Sara began thoughtfully. 'While I was shaking hands with people, I thought I heard Madame Gouvan say something to you about my grandfather?'

He hesitated for a moment. 'I – I don't remember.'

'I heard her say his name, then I thought

she mentioned something like – "it was terrible about the body?" '

'With everybody chattering in there, it was virtually impossible to hear what she was saying.'

His too-casual tone made Sara suspect he was keeping something from her. Her mind began to mull over the strange feeling she'd had in the shop, caused more by intuition than reasoning – that the villagers of Laffeine were, perhaps, over-eager in their show of friendship.

'Steve, don't you think it a little peculiar that these people have tended a stranger's grave so meticulously all these years? It has been looked after so beautifully, and yet, there were other graves without flowers and with weeds creeping over them.'

'Of course it isn't peculiar,' he replied quickly. 'Naturally they would want to preserve the memory of an Allied soldier, one who was killed in their village.'

'I suppose so.'

'How suspicious you are. Don't you believe in basic human kindness?'

'You are going to think I'm even more suspicious when I tell you – I think we are being followed.'

'Who? Where?' Steve asked, looking

round.

'On the other side of the road. Do you see that man with dark glasses and a walking-stick? In spite of his limp, he kept up with us all the way through the village. When we came out of the shop he was there again – watching.'

Steve laughed. 'He's probably some harmless old bloke, who would love to come over and talk to you like the others, but he's too shy.'

'That's the last thing he looks!'

Chapter Nine

WHEN Sara reached the château she decided to take a stroll before lunch. It was gloriously sunny and she had not yet seen the grounds properly. She stood shading her eyes on a balustraded terrace.

The scene spread out before her was delightful. A wide path bordered by limes led towards the wood between lawns dotted with buttercups and daisies. In the distance, she could see Pascal on a ladder cutting the top of a yew hedge. A few peacocks paraded in all their exotic pride, while some ducks had left the lake and were waddling across the grass.

'Mademoiselle!' a childish voice cried.

Sara skipped down the steps to the garden and walked to where Mary Betts and Michael were sitting near the shrubbery fronting the wood. Michael ran towards her and hurled his small body into her arms.

'Why don't you make Sara a necklace?' Mary suggested.

Pleased at the idea, Michael ran over to where the daisies grew thickest.

'He is a very affectionate little boy,' Sara remarked.

'Sometimes. Sometimes he is very clinging, and at others he seems to resent being touched. It is all very understandable, though . . .' She stopped, a flush spreading across her cheeks.

'I know about Michael's mother leaving,' Sara said quietly. 'Steve told me.'

'Then you will understand about Michael.'

'Did you know Mrs Clare long?' Sara asked.

'A fair time. I was working as a nanny in Scotland when I met her. She came over to Portree on holiday when she was pregnant.

The child I had been looking after was old enough to go away to school, so she asked me if I should like to come to France and care for her baby when it was born. I was very thrilled, of course – and very grateful.'

Looking at Mary Betts, Sara saw she had a kind, compassionate expression – the sort of woman with whom all secrets would be safe. The perfect nanny.

'Crystal is in a hurry,' Mary said then, turning her head.

Sara looked too, and saw the maid who was pregnant, hurrying towards them.

'Does her husband work at the château?' Sara asked.

'Crystal is not married.'

'Telephone, Mademoiselle Betts,' Crystal called. 'They will ring back in a few minutes.'

'I can look after Michael,' Sara volunteered, as Mary was about to call him.

She watched Mary's slim figure as it disappeared in the direction of the château, but Crystal stood looking at Pascal as he sliced with his shears.

'You speak English well,' Sara remarked with a smile.

'Oh – thank you.' She smiled back at Sara. 'It was compulsory at school.'

Crystal made her way back to the château and Sara turned to watch Michael. He was engrossed in making his daisy-chain.

'That's lovely,' she said. The moment the words were out of her mouth she could have kicked herself for disturbing him.

He threw the daisies in the air and with a look of devilment on his face, charged into the wood.

Sara raced after him. But as she entered a thicket, he was nowhere to be seen. She knew he was hiding. He was only a little boy and he could not have run far.

'Michael,' she called, trying to sound casual. There was no reply and no sound except birds singing. She felt a tightening in her throat. 'Michael!'

She darted from tree to tree. 'Michael, please, come out now.'

Don't worry, she told herself, he won't be far away. She went deeper into the wood, her eyes searching. Suddenly, she started and drew in her breath.

Pascal had appeared from behind a huge oak tree and was face to face with her. He was still holding his big shears and the muscles in his arms were like huge knots. Sweat was shining on his brown skin.

'I will help you look for the boy,' he said.

She glanced round. They were quite alone. She felt incredibly nervous.

'Th . . . thank you, Pascal. But I think I can manage. He won't have gone far.'

He began to massage the nobbly bark of the tree trunk. 'I think we go together. *Oui?*'

She swallowed. 'I'll find him,' she said firmly.

He changed his shears from one hand to the other. 'It is best I show you where he hides. The lake – it is dangerous.'

'Oh, my God . . . the lake!' she cried. 'Michael! Michael!'

She had started to run with Pascal close beside her when a small, mischievous face peeped out at them from behind a bush. '*Bonjour*, Mademoiselle.'

Sara stared at Michael. She was breathing heavily.

Pascal murmured. 'He is OK.'

Sara took the boy's hand very firmly in hers. They stood together while Pascal ambled away. She could not make up her mind if she had done him an injustice to be so nervous of his presence. Steve had hinted that she was unduly suspicious of people. And she did believe in human kindness. But . . . Pascal had such a strange, staring

59

expression . . .

'I'm tired,' Michael declared, pulling against her hand.

She bent down. 'Come on, scamp, I'll give you a piggy-back.'

Michael scrambled up on her back, squealing.

Sara ran with him across the wood towards the lawns. Then she stopped and a guilty flush suffused her face.

In the clearing ahead stood Jules Clare. He waited for her, tall and straight like a statue. She prepared herself for the coming onslaught. She could hear him now. Why did she go rampaging through his wood like a wild bull?

To her absolute astonishment, she saw the flicker of a smile on his face. It had to be for Michael, of course.

He moved towards them quickly and in a moment was by their side. There was only concern on his face. 'My son is heavy for you – *non*?'

'Not really,' she answered with a meekness that surprised her.

He lifted Michael down gently. 'Go to Mary now, she is waiting for you.' He looked at Sara as his son raced away. 'He is, what you say? Full of beans!'

She laughed lightly. 'A little hyperactive perhaps. How long has he . . .?' Her question trailed off as she noticed his darkening expression. She might have known Michael's unpredictable behaviour would have stemmed from the time his mother had deserted him. Jules would obviously not want to be reminded of it.

'He is a lucky boy having such a beautiful home,' she said, hoping to change the subject.

'Indeed he is. It was not always so attractive here. During the war the château was occupied by the Germans. It was completely ransacked. My mother returned to find even the doors ripped off – and hens clucking in the bedrooms. Everything had to be built up again from scratch. Fortunately much of the valuable plate had been buried in the grounds.'

'It must have been terrible.'

'It was – but the people of Laffeine counted themselves fortunate to be left alive. In one village – Oradour – the entire population was wiped out by Hitler's SS in a way I will not describe to you. Stories that have been handed down and will never – must never – be forgotten. Those atrocities must not be allowed to happen – ever again!' There was a fierceness in his clear blue eyes that startled Sara.

It made her realise how far apart their worlds were. She had never known the tragedy of war – even her grandfather, who had been killed, was someone she only knew through her parents.

Jules must have been born at the end of the war when it was all still painfully alive. He would have grown up at a time when the sores were healing. It made more of a chasm between them than their age.

After lunch, Sara was crossing the hall when Madame Darle smiled at her. 'You found the grave of your grandfather last night, Mademoiselle?'

'I did, thank you.'

Madame Darle nodded. 'Then you must be very pleased.'

'I was – until the poachers nearly shot me,' Sara declared ruefully. She noticed with surprise that all the colour had drained out of the housekeeper's face at her remark. The woman suddenly seemed much older. She commiserated with Sara then, after a pause, gave a forced smile. 'And now you have found what you came for, I suppose you will be leaving us?'

Her question puzzled Sara. Steve had said how much pride she took in her standards of hospitality. How she cosseted guests at the château, often persuading them to stay longer than they had intended. Yet, here she was speaking of Sara leaving.

Sara felt hurt and, instead of replying that she would be going as soon as her car was ready, she heard herself saying, 'I don't know when I shall be leaving, Madame Darle. Laffeine is such a fascinating place and I have been meeting such interesting people.

'Madame Narbon has invited me to supper one day – she was very busy in the shop and there was not enough time to talk about my grandfather for long. But, of course, I will let you know when I decide to go.'

Madame Darle inclined her head politely and walked silently away.

Later, Sara stood in the quiet of the small, family chapel. She had discovered it while exploring the château that afternoon. It was a real haven of peace – the only one it seemed in this place where there was an undercurrent of uneasiness everywhere. Suddenly, she heard footsteps behind her on the marble floor. She turned quickly.

Jules Clare was walking towards her. 'I saw the door open and wondered who was in here,' he told her.

'I – I'm sorry. I should have asked first.'

'*Non*. As a guest you are free to go anywhere.'

She thanked him. She wondered why his presence always made her nervous. And his present courtesy made her more apprehensive than his displeasure. He was strangely formal, although his handsome, rugged features were not set so sternly as usual.

'I hear from Steven that you are something of a celebrity, Mademoiselle? He has just told me you are the granddaughter of the British soldier killed here in the war?'

'Yes – I came to Laffeine to see his grave.'

There was a long silence between them. A soft sunlight drifted in through the windows.

When Jules spoke at last there was a new gentleness in his tone she had not heard before.

'I . . . I think I may have been a little harsh last night.'

She hid a smile. Was this the nearest he could come to an apology? 'I should not have been in the wood,' she replied softly.

'You have more right than most.'

'Monsieur?' She glanced at him inquiringly.

'It was in the wood that your grandfather was shot down by the Gestapo. Had it not been for men like him we might not have had our freedom today.'

The thought that she might have crossed the very spot where her grandfather had fallen was shattering to Sara.

'How do you know this?' she asked.

'It is common knowledge in Laffeine. There were other deaths here – men and women in the Resistance, but only one British soldier was killed in this village.'

He stretched out his arm and his long fingers touched her arm lightly. 'You may stay in my home as long as you like.'

The gesture stunned her into silence. There were questions she wanted to ask. Something Steve had hidden from her. But she could only stand and watch as Jules left the chapel. There was a tingling in her arm.

She went to her room feeling curiously happy. She was aware she was basking in reflected glory, but she didn't care. Jules Clare respected her. Because of her grandfather she was an honoured guest in his

65

château.

She caught sight of herself in the mirror. Her cheeks were flushed, strands of hair curled across her forehead. She opened her drawstring shoulder-bag to take out her comb. On top of her belongings was a folded piece of paper. Curiously, she unfolded it and read the words scrawled there.

She did not need much knowledge of French to translate it, even obscene French. Someone was threatening to do dreadful things to her if she did not leave Laffeine. Immediately!

Chapter Ten

ANYONE in the château could have dropped the note in her bag. Sara knew that. But why? Who could hate her enough to threaten her in such vile manner if she did not leave?

She bit her lip and frowned. Suppose it had nothing to do with hate? Perhaps it was fear that had driven someone to these terrible lengths. She tried to reason it out.

Here she was, a summer tourist, enjoying a well-earned holiday in France and visiting her grandfather's grave at the same time . . . and she was unearthing memories that had lain dormant for over forty years! Perhaps there was someone who did not want to remember what had happened in Laffeine all those years ago.

Her hands were shaking as she smoothed out the crumpled piece of paper she had furiously crushed in the palm of her hand. She read it again and paled.

For a while she sat perfectly still, staring at the sun as it streamed in through the open windows. Suddenly, she jumped up, her lips set in a tight line. Her decision made, she tore the note into tiny pieces.

Sighing then, she crossed to the window. She heard a faint noise behind her and, startled, she turned quickly. An enormous red ball was rolling across the cream carpet towards her, then she spotted Michael's tousled hair as he peeped round the door before running away.

She gave a short laugh and told herself grimly that the note was already having its effect. She picked up the ball and tossed it into the air. This movement and the sight of the child helped to relax her.

She hurried to look for Michael. It was unusual for him to be unsupervised in this part of the château, but he was nowhere to be seen as she searched the dim passages. Then she heard somebody talking in whispers. The sound seemed to bounce against the walls and echo round the dark corners.

'No, Monsieur!' a woman's voice exclaimed.

Suddenly, Sara saw Steve at the end of the passage with the maid, Crystal. He was talking earnestly and holding her arm. When they saw Sara, Crystal hurried away, an anxious expression on her pretty face.

Sara felt embarrassed to be an intruder on the scene.

Steve strolled casually towards her. 'She's frightened of her own shadow that one. You'd think I was trying to eat her instead of merely asking a few simple questions.'

'She didn't appear to be in the mood to answer them,' Sara replied dryly.

'Oh, she is a silly girl.'

'She's pregnant and probably more easily upset at the moment,' Sara said gently. She noticed then that Steve looked strained. 'Are you all right?'

'Just a bit tired, that's all, I haven't been

sleeping so well. I've never realised before how many creaks and groans this château has at night. And I've been having odd dreams about . . .' He stopped.

'About what?'

He shrugged. 'It sounds daft – but I've been waking up in the night with the feeling my aunt is still here.'

'But you know she's left. You told me that yourself. Supposedly with her lover.'

'That's what everyone wants us to think, isn't it? Look, why don't we go to my room for a few minutes? It's easier to talk. Unless you want to go out and play ball, of course?'

She laughed and tossed the ball to him. 'I was looking for Michael.'

Sara had expected that Steve's room would have all the trappings of a student, but this had even more. As the door was opened and shut, a mobile made of sea-shells chinked lightly in the breeze. Twenties-style posters adorned the walls and in one corner was a stack system with an assorted range of music.

She was interested to see a flute lying in a corner – but what surprised her more was to see a set of runes and a pendulum on a cord.

Sara picked up the pendulum. 'What's

69

this?'

'Have you heard of a sixth sense? Animals have it – they can often sense approaching disasters. Well, I believe it is in human beings, too – waiting to be tapped.'

'How?'

'You simply relax the brain and let the subconscious take over. Allow impressions to seep into the mind while you swing the pendulum.'

'What impressions?'

'Impressions, Sara, that lie in the very foundations of buildings.' Steve's voice grew quieter. 'People have lived in this old château for centuries. Their hopes and fears – their happiness and their nightmares are trapped for ever in its very fabric waiting to be brought to life again. By you . . . by me. By anyone who is not afraid of the unknown.'

There was something about his eyes that made Sara put the pendulum down. She moved over to look at a photograph on his dressing-table instead. It was of a stunningly beautiful woman.

She found it difficult to tell the woman's age. Age was of little importance to Sara. When she met someone, they either attracted her by their warmth and kindness

70

or isolated her from them by a cold manner.

But in any case, this woman was an enigma. Although she was baby-faced with pink cheeks and pouting lips, there was a lifetime of experience in her sultry, green eyes.

'Who is this?' she asked.

'Aunt Helen,' Steve answered. 'She was my last remaining relative. I suppose it made a sort of bond between us.'

It was the second time he had referred to his aunt in the past tense, she noticed.

Steve looked at her earnestly. 'Nothing makes sense. I'm sure she would have contacted me. And it is unbelievable that she's never been back to see Michael. She spoiled him rotten when she was here . . . absolutely adored him.'

'Were the police informed when she left?'

'Not to begin with. She left Jules a note saying she was leaving him.'

'Well . . .'

'It still doesn't make sense! The police must think so, too. They often come to the château to see Jules and sometimes they question the servants to see if anyone has heard anything more of Helen. A fat lot of good that will do. They close ranks on the police.'

'Steve, what do you think has happened to her?'

He chose his words carefully. 'I don't know yet, but I'm working on it. I'm determined to find out, of that you can be sure. The night she left I heard her quarrelling with Jules. Just now I was trying to find out what Crystal knows, but it was useless – the girl seemed too scared out of her wits to say anything. I'm sure she knows something about that night – she was my aunt's personal maid at the time.'

He was silent for a few minutes, rubbing at his forehead with his fingers. 'Sometimes . . . sometimes I wonder if Jules wanted Helen out of the way.'

'Steve, that's a dreadful thing to say!' Sara was astonished by his words. 'Why should he?' she asked then, curiosity overcoming her surprise.

'Well, he has never lacked for admiration from women, though for the life of me I can't imagine what it is they see in him – even servants like Crystal . . .' His voice trailed off as if he was half-afraid to say what he was thinking.

'At the time Helen left,' he continued after a pause, 'I used to think he spent an inordinate amount of time closeted in his study with that secretary of his. He certainly neglected his wife.'

Sara was horrified now at what he was hinting. 'You can't possibly mean he would do anything to her? What about the letter she left?'

'A typed letter with her signature. Come on, Sara – he's a writer – he would have no difficulty deceiving anyone with a forged letter.'

Sara sat in a chair and studied Steve. There was little doubt in her mind that he was overwrought. Tiredness could cause that. His judgement must have been affected for him to try to incriminate Jules. She only hoped he had said nothing of this to anyone else in the château.

She tried to sound casual and light-hearted. 'Come on, Steve – neither of us has any experience of marriage personally and it is impossible to tell what happens in other people's private lives. No one can apportion blame as to why Jules and Helen split up. Partners run away from marriage for lots of reasons – and perhaps now your aunt can't face coming back to see Michael simply because it would be too painful.'

Steve flopped down on the bed. 'Thank

you, Teacher!'

She flushed deeply. 'I'm sorry but you seemed so convinced . . .'

'She is trying to get in touch with me, Sara.'

Sara stared. 'What?'

'She is here. I know it.' He started swinging the pendulum round very slowly. He seemed to forget Sara was there in the room. Gradually, his expression became dreamy and distant, his eyelids heavy.

At first, Sara had an urge to laugh but then she felt a prickling down her spine. Suddenly, the room seemed to be growing icy-cold.

'Steve,' she cried, dropping on the bed to sit beside him. 'Are you a witch or a wizard or something?'

Steve was fully alert and grinning then. 'I told you – it's all to do with insight.'

She was growing tired of his mystical explanations – and a little nervous. 'All right,' she said, forcing a smile. 'Give me an insight into who the pervert was who dropped a letter into my bag telling me what he – or she – was going to do to me if I didn't leave Laffeine today.'

He stared. 'You can't be serious!'

'As serious as you are about your aunt,'

she assured him.

'For heaven's sake, why didn't you tell me before? Where is this letter?'

'I tore it up.'

'I knew there was something wrong here this summer. I knew it! There has to be a lunatic wandering about the place – someone who's mentally unbalanced, but appears normal on the surface.'

Sara glanced around her at all the trappings designed to help Steve slide into a trance-like state. 'I – I think I'll go and get ready for supper.'

He caught hold of her arm. 'No, Sara, it wasn't me who sent the note.'

'I – I didn't for one minute—'

'You did.' He sprawled backwards on the bed and tucked his hands under the nape of his neck.

'Of course, I didn't,' she protested.

'Then prove it . . . Come to bed with me.'

Her jaw dropped in astonishment.

He appraised her figure. 'You're damned attractive you know! No, I don't think you do realise. Strange – the women at college are only too aware of their looks. But with hair like yours and a figure—'

'Steve!' she interrupted him, half-embarrassed, half-annoyed.

His expression became jauntily impudent. 'You're scared. Or is it that Matthew wouldn't like it?' he teased.

She stood up. 'Doesn't your sixth sense tell you the reason?'

He sighed. 'You are missing the opportunity of a lifetime.'

At this, she burst into laughter. 'No one can ever accuse you of having an inferiority complex.' She moved towards the door.

His change of mood made her look back quickly at him.

'Sara' – he was sitting upright again, his expression deadly serious – 'don't ignore the note you got. Get out of this place now. If you have to stay in France, go to another village. I'm not sure yet what's going on here – but my advice is – go!'

Steve's words stuck in Sara's mind. She was aware that one of her faults was obstinacy; always reacting stubbornly to pressures she thought were unreasonable. Everyone had the right to their own free choice. But she asked herself, in this case, could it become dangerous for her here if she refused to leave Laffeine?

Common sense told her Steve was right. After all, she had nothing to stay for. She had seen her grandfather's grave which was why she had come in the first place, but she would have enjoyed hearing about him from the people he had known in the village.

She was still deep in thought as she walked down the winding stone staircase. She had just reached the halfway landing when from above her came a shattering clatter.

She instinctively jumped to one side and grabbed the wrought-iron balustrade when a blur of black and blue metal hurtled past her on the stairs. It crashed against the moulded panelled walls. Sara stared as Michael's pedal car rolled on to its side like a lifeless body.

'Michael!' a panic-stricken voice screamed. The normally calm Mary Betts seized hold of Michael as he was about to make a run from the top of the stairs. 'You naughty, naughty boy! You might have hurt Sara. You know you are never allowed to play on the stairs.'

'My car ran away!' he shouted. Then he lashed out violently and wriggled from her grasp.

'He knows he should never play—'

'I'm all right. Really,' Sara assured her. She noticed how white Mary's face was in spite of the fact she had been running.

'Mary, what's wrong?' Sara asked, going forward to meet her.

'It's only a headache.' Mary shook her head slightly.

But Sara noticed her eyes were red, too.

'I've had some bad news,' Mary said then. 'My mother is very ill. If there's no improvement soon, I must go home.'

Her words brought a terrible ache to Sara. She had thought she was getting over her own mother's death, but the words she'd just heard brought all the sadness and hurt back.

She touched Mary's arm gently. 'I'm sorry, Mary. Can I do anything? What about Michael?'

'Monsieur Clare wanted me to take the evening off, but there was no point. I needed to keep busy. But now—'

'Please,' Sara insisted gently, 'go and rest. I'll look after the boy.'

Chapter Eleven

SARA found Michael more demanding than

a class full of children. But soon he was tucked up in bed wearing his spaceman pyjamas and clutching a cuddly bear. She began to read to him.

He listened intently, sucking his thumb and staring at the bright pictures. Suddenly, he jabbed his small finger at one of them; it was a plump, homely woman in a checked apron, taking a steaming pudding out of the oven.

'That's my mummy,' he declared.

When he was asleep, Sara stroked his hair lightly. Suddenly, she felt a deep compassion for him. She turned quickly as the door opened.

Jules entered softly. 'I was hoping to catch him before he fell asleep,' he whispered. He bent to kiss his son, then turned to Sara. 'I wonder if we might talk, Mademoiselle? In my study perhaps?'

The study was a spacious room on the ground floor. The first thing Sara noticed was an imposing mahogany desk with panelled sides and deep drawers. The word processor looked quite out of place to Sara, as she glanced at the rest of the antique furniture.

Jules beckoned her to sit down and then lowered his long, lean body into a chair opposite her.

'I expect you are wondering the reason for this meeting, *non*?' he said.

Sara found the formality between host and guest somewhat pompous, but she said nothing. She noticed his well-formed lips were set in a firm line.

Only once had she seen the hint of a smile on them.

'My son's nanny has personal problems,' he was saying. 'I have decided she must fly home immediately.' He stood up and walked to the windows where he stared out at the early evening sky.

Sara wondered what Mary Betts could have to do with her?

'I hear my son misbehaved tonight,' he said suddenly. 'That he might have hurt you.'

'Oh – what happened was an accident, I'm sure.'

'Nevertheless, he will be severely reprimanded tomorrow.'

'No!'

He turned slowly. 'Excuse me?' he said coldly.

'Little children are like puppies – you must scold them at the moment of naughtiness – like Mary did. By tomorrow, Michael

80

will almost have forgotten. His energies will be concentrated on other things. That's the time to guide him forward, not drag him backwards.'

'Really, Mademoiselle?' There were little blue flames flickering in his eyes. 'I disagree with you. Michael's intelligence is not to be compared to that of a puppy. He will remember very well, I can assure you. And I can promise you it will not happen again. He knows he is not allowed to play on the stairways.'

'Is that what you wanted me for? To tell me that?'

'No, it was not.'

There was a long silence between them. He was an overbearing man, Sara decided, self-contained, and with no room for the opinions of others. For a short time in the chapel, she had wondered if she had judged him too harshly, but now . . .

'I wanted to ask you . . .' He suddenly seemed reluctant to come to the point. 'It is this – while Miss Betts is away from Laffeine, Madame Darle is able to look after Michael for part of the day, but there are times when household commitments prevent this. I am therefore looking for a responsible person who would agree to take on a temporary . . .'

'You want me to look after him?' Sara gave a surprised laugh.

'You handle him very well – and as your car is still not repaired, I thought you might . . .'

Her thoughts were confused. Under normal circumstances she would have jumped at the opportunity of extending her stay at the château and getting to know Michael better. No child could be so cruelly deprived of a parent without it having some effect and she already felt a fondness for him. But she could not get the note out of her mind – and Steve's advice to leave now.

Jules was looking down at her with a softer expression. 'I . . . I think you would be good for Michael.'

'In spite of my views on children disagreeing with yours?' She grinned.

'Oh, we are not at all different where the fundamentals are concerned.'

'Which are?'

His voice was low. 'To care. To love.' The sensuous, heavy-lidded eyes studied her closely. An emotion she could not name surged through her.

Later, she convinced herself that she had only agreed to stay because she owed it to her grandfather as his only living relative to find out all she could about his death, just in the same way she supposed Steve had to find out about his aunt.

'Very well – I'll help until Mary Betts comes back.'

'Excellent!' He shook her hand. His grip was warm and firm. She avoided looking into his eyes again and instead glanced beyond him to the portraits on the wall.

'My parents,' he said, following her gaze.

'They were very attractive.'

'And happy together – the short time they had.'

'Was it the war?'

'*Oui*. My father was in the army. In nineteen-forty he was in the front line. After the Belgian surrender he was in one of the units covering the British evacuation of Dunkirk – fierce, bloody, rearguard fighting. Most of his comrades were killed, but he was wounded and captured by the enemy: he managed to escape later, but was killed near the end of the war, working for the Resistance.'

'I'm so sorry.'

He went to sit near her. She noticed the sprinkling of grey near his temples. He leaned forward, his elbows on his knees, his hands clasped.

'My mother went to her cousin when she heard Germans were using the château for headquarters. She helped many refugees who were cramming the roads at the beginning of the war and being strafed and bombed.

'She always remembered the bodies in the ditches and the red glow of houses that had been burned out. It was a disastrous time. Great areas of countryside were destroyed by troops.'

'How terrifying it must have been. I can't imagine how I would react in such a dreadful situation.'

'I hope you never have to find out. My mother said it was hard to bear the humiliation of being occupied by enemy troops.'

'British towns and cities were badly bombed, but thank God we weren't invaded.'

'Surprising the Germans did not plunge into Britain after Dunkirk. Their forces were very powerful and it's doubtful that Britain would have been able to withstand them at that time. After that, of course, she grew steadily stronger. Fortunately for you – but not for France – the Germans turned south.'

'You know so much about the war,' Sara remarked, surprise in her voice.

'From my mother's diaries as well as all she told me. Any writing ability I have, comes from her.'

'Did . . . did your wife write as well?' she ventured.

'A little – at times.'

She immediately dropped the subject when she saw the expression on his face. 'If your parents were not in Laffeine during the war, they would not have known of my grandfather then?'

'Oh, everyone heard about the British soldier who was shot here.'

After a pause, Sara plucked up her courage and faced him squarely. 'Will you please tell me what happened to him – after they shot him?'

His eyes were questioning. 'But I thought you knew. You went down to the village, spoke to many people . . .'

'No one told me. Please, Jules.' It was the first time she had addressed him by his first name. It slipped out. She was not sure if he liked it. 'Please tell me. I would rather hear the truth from you than some garbled version from someone else.'

For a moment, she thought he was going

to refuse.

He frowned and said nothing, then he nodded briefly. 'You have the right to know, of course. But I warn you, it is not pleasant. Shall I go on?'

She pressed her lips together nervously and nodded.

He spoke quietly. 'After your grandfather was shot in the wood, the Germans dragged his body to the village square. They . . . they crucified him . . .' He stopped. 'That is all I know.'

She swallowed. 'How long did he take to die?'

'I do not know. There was a guard on him all the time. No one could help him.'

'Did anyone try?' she asked coldly.

'It is very easy to say that without a gun in your back,' he replied soberly. 'Yes, they tried – and suffered for their courage.'

She hung her head. She had never felt so ashamed. 'I'm sorry. I should not have said that.' She stood up and walked to the door.

'I'm sorry you had to hear this,' he said then.

'Oh, no,' she answered quickly. 'I'm grateful to you for telling me. You see, I want to find out all I can about my grandfather's experiences in Laffeine – and I am sure there is something more that has not yet been told. Something someone wants hidden.'

He frowned. 'Why do you say such a thing? Why should you imagine—'

'Not imagination, I assure you. I've had a note dropped into my shoulder-bag today – by a person who is very anxious that I leave the village – and has even threatened me if I don't. It can only be because I am reviving old memories.'

His astonishment was apparent. 'But this is not possible. It must be a joke of some sort.'

'I didn't find it very amusing,' she told him briefly.

'Where is the letter? Show me.'

Suddenly, she felt very foolish. 'I tore it up. I thought it was the best thing to do with it.'

'You tore it up?' he echoed with disbelief. 'So now you have no proof that such a note existed?' He sighed deeply. 'You were unwise. Such a letter would be better in police hands, even if it were the work of a crank – which I suspect.'

'No, I'm sure someone in the château wants me out of the way,' Sara insisted.

He shook his head vehemently. '*Non*! No

87

one in my home would ever do such a thing. It is obviously the work of an outsider. You have been to the village. Anyone could have dropped it in your bag.'

She knew by the set of his mouth there was no point in contradicting him. There was a deep frown on his face.

'You should have told me about this before,' he said. 'Perhaps it would not be such a good idea for you to stay here after all.'

Sara was furious at his last remark. 'I shall leave when I am ready and not because some lunatic is trying to intimidate me.'

His expression altered. She even wondered if she saw a smile at the corners of his lips.

'I think our crank writer must beware the tigress that bites,' he said solemnly.

Was he referring to her ability with the martial arts? she wondered. She felt a twinge of discomfort. Why did he have the power to make her feel unfeminine? Perhaps he preferred the women around him to be timid creatures?

There was a light knock at the door and an attractive blonde woman entered. She was dressed in a tight, navy skirt and chic white shirt that managed to reveal the beginnings of a milk-white cleavage. She made Sara feel gauche and overdressed.

Jules introduced his secretary, Matilde, who smiled sweetly as she shook hands then went to sit demurely at the desk.

As Sara left the room she wondered if the woman were a workaholic that she should come to Jules so late in the day. Then she scolded herself for unkind thoughts.

Chapter Twelve

OVER the next few days, Sara found that looking after Michael was both tiring and rewarding; he was happiest when fully occupied and she tried to make sure when he was with her that he was supplied with plenty of activity.

One morning Steve stopped her in the hall. 'Thank your lucky stars you don't have to work in the kitchen,' he said with a grin. 'There's all hell let loose in there. Two of the maids are down with colds. Crystal is sick, Madame Darle is going spare because the meat hasn't been delivered, and she can't get in touch with Pierre because his phone is out of order. The cook—'

'Where is Michael?' Sara asked, interrupting him anxiously.

'Uncle Steve is playing the Good Samaritan and taking him fishing.'

'Well, do you think it might help if I went down the village and asked about the meat? I really wanted to see Pierre and Claudette some time, if only to jog their memories. They were going to ask me to their house to talk about my grandfather.'

'I should think Madame Darle would be delighted.'

'Not delighted, Steve,' Sara said wryly. 'I don't think she likes me very much.'

'Nonsense! She's a reserved sort of person – and could probably give that impression. But I'm sure she'll be only too pleased to take you up on the suggestion.'

Steve was right. Madame Darle's tight-lipped politeness was no longer evident. But even so, Sara felt a peculiar uneasiness with her. The older woman's grateful smile did not extend to her grey eyes.

This time, Sara did not decline the use of Jules' car.

'Pascal will drive you to the village,' Madame said.

'Oh – no, there is no need to trouble

him.'

'But it is no trouble.'

'Really – I would like to drive myself.' Sara did not wish to offend the woman, but neither did she relish the idea of sitting beside Pascal.

'As you wish. He will take it to the front drive for you.'

'Right. Now, Madame, what sort of meat did you order?'

Sara looked at the clothes in her wardrobe with some dissatisfaction. They were all colourful and summery – but somehow, not very – chic. When she had a free day perhaps she would go to one of the nearby towns and buy something that was more tailored.

'I shall wear my flowered skirt,' she said aloud, finally making a decision. Then she chose a plain white blouse to go with it.

At the last minute she put on a white straw boater she had bought specially for her holiday.

When she reached the drive she saw Steve admiring a sleek, coffee-coloured Porsche parked there. 'You must be well in favour, Sara,' he remarked, smiling. 'This is Jules' latest.'

She hesitated before getting into it. 'Do you suppose Pascal has brought the wrong car round?'

'Not on your life. He wouldn't dare to touch this one without permission. It must have been Jules' suggestion. For goodness' sake, don't scratch this baby.'

Steve was totally unaware that he was making Sara more and more nervous.

She glanced at the car dubiously. 'I – I think I would rather take one of the old ones.'

'What old ones? None of Jules' cars is more than two years old.'

She climbed very carefully into the driving seat and felt a shiver of excitement down her spine. She had never driven such a car. Then she spotted Jules in the distance. She was sure he was watching her. Excitement turned to apprehension, but in no way was she going to climb out and show him she could not handle his new toy.

Sara switched on the engine and, after waving good-bye to Steve, began to drive very slowly in the direction of the big double gates.

Once out of sight of Jules she was able to relax, and found the car a dream to handle. She told herself that one day, when she was rich, she would buy such a car. They were made for each other. She sighed contentedly as they glided along the sunny country lanes. She began to sing softly.

Then she caught a movement from the corner of her eye – something on the floor of the car near her feet.

Seconds later, a khaki-coloured snake, with an arrow pattern on its head, slithered out from under the passenger seat.

Chapter Thirteen

SARA had a sheer terror of snakes of any sort – even harmless grass snakes. Their sliding, slippery-looking appearance filled her with shuddering revulsion. She knew that this snake, with the zig-zag pattern along its back would have glands that secreted poison. Every muscle in her body seemed to contract and she felt as if she were frozen to her seat.

Very slowly, she managed to ease her foot from the accelerator. She was petrified in case she made any jerky movement, causing the reptile to strike out at her with its fangs.

Despite her fear, she wondered fleetingly how she could feel so cold and be sweating at the same time.

She was almost mesmerised as the snake began to wriggle up the side of the passenger seat, twisting like some exotic, oriental dancer. Her heart seemed to swell, filling her chest, shaking her body with its thunderous beat.

She struggled to regain control of herself. A tiny voice of reason inside her ordered her to stay calm. She told herself that there were serums to combat venom, that there was no point in complicating the already horrific issue by becoming panic-stricken and giving herself a heart attack as well. Very gradually her pulse lessened its pumping action.

The reptile slithered into a neat coil on the passenger seat.

Sara forced her left hand to move slowly from the driving wheel towards her head. She told herself repeatedly that she must not make any sudden movement.

She knew that what she was going to do next was liable to cause the car to swerve, and she prayed for an empty road. She was also going to trust her reactions to be quicker than they had ever been.

Her hand touched her head and in a flash

she had whipped the straw boater from her head and brought it down over the viper.

The Porsche rolled uneasily from side to side as Sara tried to control the wheel with one hand and hold down the hat with the other. As she leaned sideways, rivulets of perspiration ran down her back. She could not imagine what she was going to do once she had brought the car to a halt.

She decided later it had to be Fate – however revolting the next few minutes turned out to be – that decreed she was going to have company for the rest of the journey.

She saw a van parked at the side of the road several yards ahead of her and a woman waving to her from the verge. In spite of the grim situation in which she found herself, an ironic smile touched her lips. Would the woman be so keen to thumb a lift with her if she knew what Sara had in the car beside her?

She drew up as smoothly as she could. A moment later, she recognised Louise, the butcher's assistant, peering in through the car window. The older woman seemed to draw back fractionally when she saw Sara, and Sara remembered how unfriendly she had been in the shop.

She tried to cry out, but her mouth felt

abnormally dry. 'There's a snake in here!' she managed at last. 'I've got it trapped under my hat. I daren't move. Can you please get help?' She was ashamed that all her courage had finally deserted her and tried to stop her knees shaking again.

Louise merely shrugged, appearing almost indifferent to Sara's predicament. 'Keep still. I shall open the door,' she said abruptly.

The offside door clicked open and Louise stared down at the hat then at Sara. 'Why do you look so frightened? It is only a snake, *n'est-ce pas?*'

'It's a poisonous one, I know!'

'When I put my hand on the hat, take yours away,' Louise ordered.

What happened after that was so abhorrent to Sara it made her feel physically sick. In one lightning movement, Louise lifted the hat, swung the snake by its tail like a whip, out of the car and smashed its head on the ground. The instant of death was an execution Sara hoped never to witness again.

'It was an adder,' Louise said casually, before picking up the dead snake and throwing it into the long grass.

Sara swallowed. 'Wh . . . where did you

learn to do that?'

'There were many such snakes on the common where I played as a child. I learned how to do this. It is – how you say – a knack. What is the matter? Are you ill?'

'I – I'm not used—'

Louise gestured with both hands and pursed her lips. 'It is certain you do not live in the country or you would have known how to handle him. Of course, there are other ways of—'

'Did your van break down?' Sara asked hastily before Louise could enlarge on what she was saying.

'*Oui* – and I must get back to the village quickly. The meat will have to be transferred to the other van.'

'Climb in, I'll take you.'

Louise dropped her hefty bulk on to the passenger seat. 'You do not look fit to drive,' she said in her forthright manner.

'I'm all right,' Sara murmured, trying to sort out her feelings of mingled relief and revulsion.

'You would have plenty to worry about if he had bitten you!'

'And I am forgetting to thank you for your help. I – I should be very grateful. Thank you.' Sara wiped her hands and gripped the steering wheel.

'You like me drive? My hands are steady.' Louise spread out her strong fingers and gazed at them proudly. 'You have a fine car here,' she continued.

'It isn't mine. It belongs to the owner of the château.'

'He is an unusual man to let his woman drive such a car.' Louise slanted a sly grin in Sara's direction.

'I'm not his woman,' Sara countered, but Louise only smirked.

Soon they were in the village and Sara drew the car on to the butcher's forecourt.

Before climbing out, Louise turned and looked at her hard. 'How did the snake get into the car?'

'I don't know. I expect it came in from the woods round the château and when the garage doors were open—'

'Hah!' Louise exclaimed contemptuously. 'It is very unlikely. Vipers prefer the heaths and commons. It is more possible he was put there deliberately.'

The remark stunned Sara to begin with, then slowly she realised it was very possible, especially after the threatening note she had received. Her mind reverted to the time she had stood by her grandfather's grave and been shot at. Everyone, including Jules, had been so insistent it must be poachers – now, Sara was equally convinced it was not. Someone was trying to kill her. But Louise's next remark made her hot with anger.

'Not everyone in a small village welcomes the stranger, Mademoiselle. Perhaps it is time for you to move on, *n'est-ce pas?*'

Sara opened the car door and jumped out. 'Thank you for your help, Louise,' she said brightly. 'You must excuse me. I have to talk to Pierre and Claudette. There are so many things I have to do in Laffeine – it just wouldn't be possible for me to move yet.' Then she slammed the door behind her.

Sara's anger at Louise's veiled threat soon turned to despondency, however. She left the butcher's shop feeling puzzled and miserable. Pierre had been like a different person. Not totally unfriendly, perhaps, but reluctant to talk to her.

He had certainly not confirmed that he and Claudette were going to invite her to their house to talk about her grandfather. He had smiled and been pleasant, but she sensed there was something wary about him now and he had pretended to be frantically busy with his few customers. There had been no sign of the warmth the couple had greeted Sara with when they had met her.

Sara was also perplexed and strangely worried by the strained expression she'd noticed on Claudette's face.

She left the car in the forecourt and walked to the other small shops, her mind fully occupied. Sara then noticed the same old man with the walking-stick who had followed Steve and herself, watching from the opposite side of the road again. Sara thought he was probably a beggar, judging by his shabby appearance.

Later, when she had finished her shopping and was about to walk back to the car, she heard a tap-tapping on the cobbles behind her. Sara decided to find out for certain if he was following her, so she turned quickly into a quiet side street.

The old man did the same.

Sara could stand this no longer, and suddenly she rounded on him. 'Why are you following me?' she demanded.

'I thought you would never slow down, Mademoiselle,' he replied calmly. 'I am not so quick as I used to be.'

Sara was puzzled by his reply. She glanced round the empty street. 'What do you want?'

'I saw you go into Pierre Narbon's shop.'

'Well?'

'He had no time for you, *non*?'

'Oh, yes, he did. He was very—'

'Very frightened?'

'Whatever do you mean?' She frowned and began to edge away from him. He might be crippled and carrying a stick, but at close quarters, with his broad shoulders and strong, wide hands, he looked quite powerful.

'If you come with me, I will tell you what I mean,' he said.

As she hurried away, she heard him chuckle.

'You have your grandfather's spirit, *ma petite*!' he called after her.

She stopped and turned round. 'What do you know about my grandfather?'

'A great deal. It was at my house he stayed.'

She stared, not knowing whether to believe him or not. There was a grin now on his brown, leathery face.

'I could tell you plenty, Sara Parish. Like, for instance – your grandmother's name was Alice May and she had hair the colour of burnished copper and the finest pair of brown eyes in the whole of England.'

A slow, exquisite smile lit up Sara's face. At last, she told herself, she had found someone who could talk to her about the man who was gradually becoming something of a legend in her mind.

'We cannot talk here,' he continued, glancing round him. 'I have written my address on this card. I will meet you there in half an hour.' He pointed a knobbly finger. 'Follow the river.'

She watched him limp along the street between the half-timbered houses and had the feeling that, like Pierre, he also did not wish to be seen talking to her for long.

From his shabby appearance, she had expected him to have a modest home and was surprised to see a large, stone farmhouse in the rolling countryside over-looking the jumble of pointed rooftops of Laffeine.

She drove the Porsche along a dirt track, passing several barns with planks of rotting wood and hens clucking fussily between bales of straw.

As the track became more bumpy, she parked the car on some grass and walked the rest of the way. The house was a hand-some building with the usual long windows and small panes of glass. Ivy covered the walls and choked the gutters whilst big mauve irises and clumps of weed cluttered the broken fence beside the path.

Outward show meant little in Laffeine and Sara knew this, but the silent, deserted appearance made her a little nervous.

She knew nothing about this old man and had taken him completely on trust. As she was wondering if she had been less than prudent to come on her own, the door swung open and he beckoned her inside.

'You would like some coffee, *oui*?' he asked, as she approached cautiously.

The aroma of freshly-ground beans was delicious and the inside of the house was comfortable and homely. Sara felt easier now and sat in the winged leather chair he had pushed towards her.

'Please tell me about my grandfather, Monsieur,' she asked eagerly.

'My name is Henri,' he said. 'You must drink your coffee while it is hot.'

She sipped the steaming black liquid. She had never tasted coffee so strong before, even here in France. Her imagination ran riot. Suppose he had laced it with something? Even poison? She had no way of . . . He was watching her closely.

'It's very good,' she murmured, but put

her cup and saucer down.

He nodded his head, sat down opposite Sara and, without any further encouragement, began to speak. 'The British soldier was escaping through France from Germany. When he reached Laffeine he was completely exhausted and half-starved . . .'

At that moment the door opened and Sara recognised the woman who entered the room. It was Madame Gouvan who had spoken to her when she had first visited Pierre's shop – the woman who had seemed so uncomfortable when Sara thanked her for caring for the grave.

Henri stood up and took off his dark glasses as he kissed Madame Gouvan.

'This is my wife, Arla,' he said to Sara.

'Oh – I didn't realise . . .'

'You thought I was a beggar, *oui*?' With no home and no family?' He laughed.

'Oh, no . . .' She blushed brightly. Madame Gouvan appeared worried. 'You were not seen coming here, Mademoiselle?'

'I . . . I don't think so.'

Arla glanced at her husband. He patted her on the cheek. 'So . . . what if she was? Remember, *ma chérie*, there was a time when you and I were afraid of nothing and no one.'

Arla caught hold of his hand. It was obvious to Sara that there was a great affection between the two elderly people. She relaxed in her chair and drank the rest of her coffee.

'Good,' Henri said with a twinkle in his eyes. 'Now you are trusting.'

Sara realised how astute he had been.

'Sergeant John Parish had escaped,' Henri continued, when Arla had sat down beside him, 'from a work camp in Germany where he had been taken when he was captured at Tobruk. He hid at our village on his way to the Spanish border. The women were in the church cleaning the brasses when they found him asleep in one of the pews. They brought him to me hidden in a donkey-cart.'

'Why?'

'Why to me? I was in the Resistance – and my house was off the beaten track. They thought he would be safe with me.' He frowned and shook his head.

Arla touched his arm gently. 'Go on, Henri.'

'We did not hide him in the barn. It was the obvious hiding place – and we had tried it before. Some of our friends in the group had been found in there by the Germans. Instead, I hid him in my attic while contacts were made with one of our number who would take him to the border.'

'Were there many in the Resistance in this village?' Sara asked.

'But, of course. It was our only salvation.'

'What was my grandfather like?'

'He was a very brave boy.'

The remark sounded odd to Sara – she realised that when he died, her grandfather had been younger than she was now. She was so eager to know everything about him. 'What did he talk about?'

'He talked of home and his wife and baby – and the camp from which he had escaped. He had been put to work in a stone quarry. With shrapnel in his leg, he walked six miles every day to the quarry. Of course, the exercise helped to strengthen his muscles and prepare him for his escape. That, and breaking flint with a sledge-hammer and pushing it on a truck to the railway.

'Unless nine tons had been split each day, no food was allowed. He told me proudly the men he worked with always managed their quota.' He grimaced. 'But it could not have been the food that gave him strength to cross so much hilly country.'

'What did they get to eat?' Sara asked.

'Each morning every five prisoners received a loaf between them. He told me how they played cards for choice of slice. There was also coffee, made from acorns. Then, in the evening, after working all day at the quarry, the men would have stew made from nettles and dandelions.'

Sara sighed. 'It sounds awful – but at least he was alive.'

'Alive? You think John Parish called that living?' Henri asked. 'Not a man such as he. His one thought was to escape back to England to his wife and child. He had survived the evacuation from Dunkirk and was given a brief leave then. It was the last time he saw his wife and child. He was sent to Egypt with his regiment and eventually was caught up in the battle for Tobruk. He lived and fought with other soldiers in a dug-out.'

'Dug-out?'

'A large hole in the earth with some corrugated iron for a roof, duckboards for feet and cardboard round the walls.'

It was a world almost beyond Sara's comprehension. This was no story she reminded herself. No make-believe. This had really happened to men who were fighting for a free world.

'Then Tobruk was overrun by the Germans and John and his friends were like rats in a trap,' Henri went on. 'When captured they were thrown into cattle trucks, driven to the coast, and packed like sardines into an old ship sailing for Italy. Then more cattle trucks. For three days and nights they were driven, never allowed out until they reached the prison camp in Germany. Can you imagine the conditions?'

'I think so,' she whispered.

'Just one of the incidents of war. Perhaps a small one compared to other atrocities.'

'And he managed to escape and come all this way only to be shot,' she said quietly.

'It should never have happened. We received a message that our man was coming to take John to the border, but before he arrived we were warned the Germans were headed for my house. That was when he made his run. He was shot in the woods of the château.'

He glanced at Arla, whose gaze had never left his face. 'I . . . we believe we were betrayed that night. By someone in the village.'

'Oh, no!' Sara exclaimed, shocked by this

108

statement.

'Possibly by someone who was even with us in the Resistance. It had happened before. Our own comrades had been captured during their missions and inter-rogated by the Gestapo. The enemy always seemed to be well informed of our move-ments beforehand.'

'That is how Henri was wounded,' Arla told Sara. 'He was with a group planning to blow up a train carrying German troops, but they ran straight into an ambush. His leg was shot to pieces.'

'And you really believe someone in Laffeine betrayed you?'

'The same person – or people – who war-ned the Germans about the British soldier hidden here. But we never managed to dis-cover who the collaborator was. It is a secret the traitor either carries with him now – or has taken with him to the grave. And . . .' His eyes held Arla's for a moment. 'And I believe it is the former,' he said at last.

'You said before that Pierre and Claudette were afraid to invite me to their house?'

He nodded grimly. 'There is talk again in the village. It has happened since you came here and started making inquiries about your grandfather. Those who have spoken to you have received terrible letters. People are nervous of what could happen to them or their families if they tell you more.'

Sara's eyes widened.

'It is said that Pierre's chickens were all found dead one morning. They were decapitated. But not by a fox. By a knife,' Henri said in a low voice.

'Oh, God! What have I done?' Sara gasped. 'It is my fault for coming—'

'You have done nothing, Mademoiselle!' Henri interrupted, looking angry. 'Except to show us that the spirit of courage we all once had is no more. We now stand by like frightened, shivering rabbits – and I count myself among the rabbits. Once I led a group of fighting men. Now I look over my shoulder to see who is watching me, in case I discover the identity of the traitor.

'But make no mistake – he is more afraid than any of us. When John Parish was betrayed, this village took the shame upon itself. Whoever the collaborator was, he must know that retribution will be great should he ever be revealed. It does not matter how many years ago the war finished.'

His eyes were bright – no longer those of an old man.

Sara saw that he was reliving a time unknown to her. A time of occupation and hardship. A time of utter degradation. At last, she thought, she was beginning to understand a little of what the war had been like for people under enemy rule. When men had died like flies. When women had wept.

'Oh, no, Henri,' she heard Arla say softly. 'There is a time when we must forget . . . and forgive.'

'Not yet, *ma chérie*,' he answered gravely. 'Not yet!'

Chapter Fourteen

SARA drove back to the château trying to unravel her thoughts. Had she found the reason everyone had been so welcoming the day she visited Laffeine with Steve? Because they were consumed with guilt? It was all wrong, she told herself. In every community there was the chance of finding someone like their collaborator.

Instead of feeling guilty, they should be proud of the courage they had shown in resisting the enemy. She wondered if she could ever have been so brave.

She had rounded the last bend, and was driving at about eighty kilometres per hour towards the château, when there was a strange cracking noise. It broke into her thoughts like a whiplash. Suddenly the car was out of control and skidding towards the verge. In that instant it seemed to Sara that a great oak tree hurled itself at her.

In the dim distance she heard the sound of the car door being opened.

Then she heard a man's voice.

'Have you any pain?'

He ran his fingers over her limbs. 'Can you feel this?'

She nodded. After that a pair of strong arms cradled her. The man wore a shirt open to the waist and she relaxed against his naked chest. The feeling of safety she experienced then made her want to stay in his arms for ever.

When Sara came round she was lying in the big, four-poster bed in her room. At first she thought she had been dreaming, but then Madame Darle leaned over her with a taut expression.

'Are you all right, Mademoiselle?'

'Yes. Just a bit of a headache. But

fine . . .' She sat up quickly then. 'The car! Oh, the car! And how did I get here?'

'It is nothing to worry about. Monsieur Jules heard you crash when he was going out shooting. He carried you to the château.'

Sara felt suddenly hot. She did not know if it was because she was afraid of Jules' reaction to the car damage – or because, although she could only remember the accident vaguely, she was able to recall with startling clarity, the feel of his body. She gave a little shiver.

'I hope you are not cold, Mademoiselle? I found for you some nice, thick pyjamas in case you were suffering from shock.'

'Oh, no – I'm not at all cold. Thank you.' Sara glanced down at her strange, roomy bed attire.

There was a light knock at the door and her heart jumped as Jules entered. He carried a chair to her bedside and sat down. 'How are you, Sara?' he asked gently.

She swallowed. 'I am so very sorry about the car!' she blurted out.

He shrugged. 'It is of no consequence. Cars are expendable, people are not. The whole thing could have been much more serious. You are a very lucky girl to be alive . . .'

As he carried on talking in an unusually calm and gentle way, Sara realised he was treating her very much as he would a child. There was certainly a difference in their ages, but not enough to warrant such a manner. She found herself wishing that Madame Darle had found her something a bit more glamorous to wear than the man-sized pyjamas.

'I don't understand why the car went out of control,' she said. 'I had no trouble at all on my way to the village – with the car, anyway.'

'It was a puncture.'

'In a new car?'

He frowned. 'We shall soon find out the reason. It is being examined now. What do you mean – you didn't have trouble with the car?'

She went on to tell him about the horrific incident with the snake. His manner and expression changed immediately. Lines creased his brow as his face darkened and his manner was no longer gentle.

'I agree with the woman Louise. It is highly unlikely that a snake would choose to enter a vehicle of its own accord. The whole thing is most disturbing. Yes, we have seen snakes in the woods, but that is where they stay – is it not, Madame?'

Madame Darle looked up, startled. 'Oh, yes, Monsieur. Certainly.'

There was a clanging from downstairs as someone pulled the doorbell.

A few moments later, Crystal entered the room, breaking the silence that had pervaded it.

'The doctor is here, Monsieur, as you requested.'

Madame Darle hurried over to Sara's bed and began to smooth her hand over the duvet, to make sure it was immaculately tidy.

Sara looked at her inquiringly.

'He is here to make sure you are quite well after the accident,' she explained.

'There is absolutely no need,' Sara protested. 'I feel perfectly well.'

'You will allow him to examine you, please,' Jules ordered.

'I think I can decide that for myself,' she countered. But he had already left the room.

The doctor said she had no concussion but told Sara to rest. To her surprise, she found no difficulty complying with his advice; she slept on and off most of the day and the night, as well.

'*Bonjour*, Mademoiselle,' a bright voice said the following morning, and Crystal brought a tray into the room containing a silver pot full of steaming coffee, crispy croissants with butter and preserves.

'Breakfast in bed – such luxury!' Sara said. She had not seen Crystal looking so cheerful before.

'It will do you good, Mademoiselle. You must be looked after.'

'I am quite recovered now, Crystal, I shall be getting up this morning.'

'But no! Monsieur Jules say—'

'I shall make my own mind up, thank you.'

There was a giggle from the doorway and Michael's curly head appeared. He ran over to Sara with a tangle of buttercups in his clenched hand.

'Oh, they are lovely, Michael,' she told him warmly.

'I shall pick you lots more when Crystal and me go for a walk,' he announced.

Sara noticed there was an expression almost of triumph on Crystal's face.

'Monsieur said I was to look after Michael until further notice. He is my responsibility now,' the maid informed Sara, looking pleased with herself.

Over the next few days, Sara felt strangely out of place in the huge château. She had insisted on getting up, but although she felt well, she was conscious that every-one treated her as if she was very fragile and liable to fall apart at any moment.

She could see little point in remaining at the château unless she was allowed to carry on with the job Jules had given her of look-ing after Michael. It seemed to her it was not only cars that were expendable! No doubt Jules thought he was making her rest after the accident, but she found the days long and lonely.

Crystal and Michael were often out, while Jules spent his days closeted in his study. Sara thought she could understand a little more why Helen might have felt neglected by her husband.

How would she have felt in Helen's place? she asked herself. Writing was the man's life; a part of him that had to be accepted by anyone who loved him – but as for any hint that he might be having an affair with his secretary, that was altogether a different matter, she decided.

She strolled on to the terrace and saw Steve sprawled on a sun-bed between the tumbling, climbing pot-plants that decorated the place so attractively. When he saw Sara, he gazed lazily in her direction, shading his eyes from the sun.

'You are a fool, Sara Parish. You know that, don't you? You haven't taken a blind bit of notice of what I've said to you.'

Sara smiled at him wryly and settled herself in one of the deep-cushioned basket-chairs. She was well aware of how concerned Steve had been when she crashed the car, but on such a glorious morning it was hard to believe it had been anything more than an accident.

'I've told you, Steve, I am not being driven away from Laffeine by hysteria. There is no proof that any of these incidents has been a deliberate attempt to – harm me.'

'You nearly said "kill," didn't you? Come on, Sara – what are you waiting for? Somebody to leap into your room waving a knife over his head? Is that when you'll take notice? Don't you honestly think there have been too many of these coincidences?'

She bit her lip and frowned. At last, she admitted quietly, 'Yes, I do. And that makes me angry. I won't be pushed.'

'God, you're obstinate! You want to go back home in one piece, don't you? What about Matthew? Don't you miss him?'

She found his question disconcerting. 'Of course, I miss him! I wouldn't be marrying him if I didn't miss him, would I?'

'Methinks she doth protest too much,' he muttered.

'He is a very nice man . . . kind and reliable and—'

'So is Pascal,' he intoned.

They sat silently for a while. Then suddenly Sara said, 'I don't like him much.'

'Who?'

'Pascal. He gives me the shivers.'

'Pascal is a good bloke. Salt of the earth. He's solid – dependable – and loyal to those he loves. You don't know him well enough.'

Sara was surprised. Steve had spent far more time in Pascal's company than she had. He ought to know the man. Perhaps her own judgements were too hasty?

She saw the muscles of Steve's arms suddenly stiffen. He sat up straight and looked beyond her. Jules came striding towards them. He was wearing tight cream trousers and an open-necked, coffee-coloured silk shirt that emphasised his rich tan and dark hair. His deep voice seemed to echo round the still patio.

'I am glad to see you looking so well,

Sara. Hello, Steve. Enjoying the sun?' He settled himself in the chair beside Sara with his knees spread and his hands on his thighs. 'I wondered if either of you would like to come with me to Paris tomorrow? I'm meeting my publisher and it's an opportunity for you both to visit the place.'

'I've been there – and so has Sara,' Steve said.

The abruptness of his reply made Sara feel awkward and uncomfortable. After all, Jules was doing them a favour, offering to drive them to Paris for the day. She wondered if Steve was sitting up at nights still, playing with runes and trying to contact his aunt. Under his slight tan, he still looked strained and gaunt.

'Certainly, she's been there,' Jules replied. 'She stayed for one night. And it was raining. That is no way to see the most beautiful city in the world. She must be seen at her best. In the sun.'

'And I suppose you can arrange that?' Steve asked sarcastically.

Sara saw Jules' eyes flash dangerously, but to her relief he laughed. 'Of course. I wouldn't take her any other time. What about it, Sara?'

'I should love to go!' she exclaimed,

feeling a new excitement swamping the boredom of the last few days. To see Paris with Jules and Steve instead of being there on her own would be quite different to sitting in a cafe watching other people enjoying themselves in groups – or couples.

'Good. And you, Steve?' Jules asked.

'Sorry. I'm afraid I've made arrangements for tomorrow. Thanks all the same, Jules.' As he stood up and sauntered away, he threw Sara a look which she understood clearly.

He was warning her not to trust herself alone with his uncle. But she chose to take no notice. There was a strange, prickling sensation on her skin as if someone were touching it lightly with pins. It was not unpleasant.

Jules nodded towards her briefly. 'I shall be ready to leave at eight sharp.'

She wondered why he had to make it sound like a business appointment.

He stood up and walked to the ornamental wall at the end of the terrace and gazed out across the grounds.

'Take enough with you for an overnight stay,' he said with his back to her.

'Oh, I thought—'

'The first day there will be mainly

business for me. No doubt you would like to do some shopping then. But I shall be free after that to show you something of Paris.'

'I – I shall look forward to it.'

He turned round, folded his arms, and smiled. 'So shall I, Sara.' He tapped the side of his head. 'One can work for too long until the thoughts won't come any more. I shall enjoy relaxing.'

From the way he spoke, she had the feeling he was going to enjoy being with her as well. It must be so, otherwise he would not have offered to take her.

'And it will do you good to be away from all this,' he continued.

'Oh, but I love it here. I have never in all my life stayed in such a magnificent place, Monsieur.'

He shrugged. '*Oui*, but I feel perhaps it is no longer safe for you – much as you are welcome to stay of course. There have been too many incidents concerning you. Everyone is worried. The snake . . . the car . . .'

'You said the accident was caused by a puncture.'

'*Oui*, but the tyre was penetrated by a bullet from a powerful rifle.'

'A rifle? Do you mean to say someone

shot at me again?' she asked, horrified.

'At the car maybe.'

She stared. 'Poachers again?' she asked sarcastically.

By way of reply he simply shrugged.

So that was why he was taking her to Paris. Not because he wanted her company, but as she was a guest in his home, he probably felt it was his duty to keep her safe!

Chapter Fifteen

SARA told herself she was going to enjoy her trip to Paris with Jules, even if he was only taking her along to keep her out of harm's way. Why should he want her for her company, anyway? He barely knew her. She ignored the slight twinge of disappointment inside her.

The next morning, she hurried out to where the silver Rolls-Royce was standing in the drive. When she saw Jules, she stopped and stared in astonishment! Then she recovered herself and climbed on to the passenger seat beside him.

He turned his head towards her and

smiled. 'It wasn't a permanent feature, you know, I do shave it off from time to time.'

She blushed. 'You . . . you look so different without your beard.'

It was the understatement of the year. He looked so attractive there was a part of her that wished uneasily he had stayed as he was and her thoughts were confused as the car glided away smoothly.

They stopped on the way to have coffee. Sitting outside under the bright orange umbrella, Sara felt she was enjoying the glorious, lazy freedom of being on holiday for the first time since she had come to the château.

A pretty waitress fussed over Jules much too obviously and wiggled her shapely hips as she walked away. But he smiled at Sara and she felt warm inside.

The views from the Paris ring-road were magnificent.

'I saw the Eiffel Tower!' she called excitedly. 'I didn't see it when I was driving myself. Nor any of this. I suppose I was too concerned with finding my way out of Paris.'

'You can come to Paris every day of your life and still see something different every time,' Jules told Sara, obviously finding pleasure in her absorption. 'But to really appreciate her delights and beauty, you must walk through her streets,' he added.

He parked the car at an impressive hotel in a beautifully-tended square in the heart of the city. Inside, it was like a fairy-tale palace where there seemed to Sara to be more staff than guests although there were plenty of people coming and going.

The plush velvet reception area where Jules was greeted with warm familiarity was a far cry from the grimy entrance hall of the small hotel where Sara had had bed and breakfast on her drive through Paris.

The visitors here, too, were of a very different calibre, she thought, as a group of passing Arabs bowed a greeting to them.

As she walked along the thickly-carpeted corridors to her suite, she felt Jules' hand lightly guiding her. It was a courtesy gesture only, but nevertheless it made her skin tingle.

Her rooms were decorated in mimosa and white, giving a bright, fresh appearance to an already sunny suite and from the wide windows, she could see the Champs-Élysées. It was all perfect. She might have guessed it would be. Jules was not the sort of man to accept anything less than perfection in anything – or anybody.

As Sara drew a comb through the silky strands of her red hair, tidying herself for lunch, she scrutinised her reflection closely. She'd noticed that Helen, in the photo in Steve's bedroom, had fair, frothy hair, giving her an ethereal quality. Her own seemed brassy by comparison. She laid down the comb and sighed.

After lunch, she left Jules with his publisher, who had joined them, deep in conversation and wandered into the wide, busy streets of Paris. It was the most fascinating place she had ever visited and she soon found herself exploring farther afield than she had intended. It was a wildly heady sensation standing at the top of the Eiffel Tower with Paris at her feet and a warm breeze blowing across her cheeks.

A man and a woman came to stand near her. They had their arms round one another and were kissing rapturously. Only Parisians would advertise their love so openly, she decided.

'Come on, pet, let's get back,' the man said in a Geordie accent.

Sara grinned. So much for her assumptions! Paris cast her spell on all comers.

She arrived back at the hotel with

presents to take home, feeling exhilarated by her tour and especially excited by one special purchase.

She was surprised to see Jules in the reception area. He strode towards her with creases across his brow as if they had been etched with a black pencil.

'Do you know what the time is?' he demanded.

'I'm sorry – I didn't expect to be this late, but–' she began.

'It's almost time for dinner. Where on earth have you been?'

His tone annoyed her. She had every right to be where she liked for as long as she liked. He was not her keeper.

'I've been having a look at Paris, if you must know; touring – shopping – all sorts of things. And what's more, I enjoyed—'

'I thought you were lost!'

She recognised a note of anxiety mixed with his anger. She swallowed. 'I can look after myself,' she said lightly.

'Oh.' His blue eyes were ice-cold. 'That hasn't been very evident up to now, has it?' There was a stinging silence between them.

'This isn't Laffeine, is it?' she asked, trying to keep her voice steady. 'I don't suppose anyone would come gunning for me in

Paris!' But the argument sounded feeble even to her ears. She knew she should have phoned to let him know where she was and why she was going to be late returning to the hotel.

Ignoring what she'd said, Jules spoke again. 'Well, you're back now. Go and change for dinner.' His manner was less brusque, but he still managed to make it sound like an order.

She climbed the stairs to her suite wishing he would stop treating her like a naughty child.

After soaking in a bath filled with foaming bubbles up to her chin, she dried herself on the hotel's soft, buttercup-coloured towels and tried out the new musky talcum powder she had bought in Paris that day. It was satin-smooth on her skin. She had used most of her spending money on that, and gifts to take home – and the peach dress! She laid it lovingly on the bed.

'Oh, *ma chérie*, it brings out all the highlights in your beautiful hair!' the matronly assistant in the shop had exclaimed. 'And see how it compliments your figure.'

Sara had seen. The shop seemed to have been built from mirrors. Were they specially made to flatter? she wondered.

She had hesitated a long time before finally buying it. She had never worn a garment that was so – revealing. Its nipped-in waist and deep, square neckline left very little to the imagination.

'You like it, M'moiselle?'

Sara's eyes had danced as she saw the new woman that was her, turning slowly in front of the mirror, shifting this way and that, hardly daring to take a deep breath.

'I'll go away and think about it,' she had said. But the dress had haunted her after that and later she had hurried back to the shop, frantic in case it had been sold.

Now she slid its silky softness over her head. And her heart beat faster.

As she walked down the long, elegant staircase to where Jules would be waiting for her, she felt as if there was a cushion of air underneath her feet. But the sudden sounds of people laughing and talking in the hotel lobby, the chink of glasses in the bar, the activity of the staff, all made her stop in her tracks.

She felt too conspicuous. She had an urge to rush back and change. But it was too late. Jules had seen her.

He was walking slowly towards the stairs.

Staring. She carried on down, her knees feeling as soft as summer butter. He did not take his eyes off her for a moment. And they spoke volumes. She did not think he would ever look on her again as a child.

As he escorted her into the dining-room, she saw several guests glance towards them. She was getting used to women casting sideways looks at Jules and tonight, especially, he was more disturbingly attractive than she had ever seen him, with a dark, impeccably-cut suit and white shirt. His figure was tall and erect, his shoulders square.

The meal, of course, was perfect. She was pleased she knew enough French by now to read the menu, and blushed when Jules nodded in approval.

'How quickly you are learning my language. I shall speak to you only in French from now on.'

She laughed and shook her head. She did not know if it felt light because she had piled her hair high, or because of the sparkling wine she was drinking.

By the time she reached the *galette au chocolat* she felt wonderful; relaxed, elegant and confident. And she was no longer in awe of Jules Clare. He was only a man like any other. Being in possession of a château and a domineering manner did not mean that he had any authority over her.

She gave a contented sigh and looked around her at the huge dining-room which was flickering with light from the red-gold haloes of candles adorning each table.

'It's just like Christmas!' she exclaimed.

Then, to her confusion, Jules threw back his head and laughed.

'I'm sorry,' he said in his deep, rich accent. 'But the remark and the dress – they do not seem to belong together.'

'What's wrong with the dress?' she asked guardedly.

'Oh, nothing. It is exquisite – and you are very . . . very lovely in it. But – until now – you were not the young woman who came with me to Paris.'

Sara did not know how to take his remark. Which woman did he prefer?

'Steve would have loved all this,' she said, changing the subject.

'I do not think Steve cares for my company at the moment. He is very temperamental.' He slanted a quick look in her direction. 'Did you know he has been dabbling with the supernatural?'

'I . . . I . . .'

'Of course you do. But I suppose everyone dabbles with such playthings, once in their lives.'

'I don't think that is how he would describe them.'

'Well, whatever – I shall be glad when his feet touch the ground again. He has been difficult lately.' He gave a short laugh. 'I prefer my ghosts to be allowed to sleep peacefully in their dusty corners.' He ran his long, brown fingers round the rim of his wineglass then without looking at her he added, 'Who do you suppose he is trying to reach?'

His question took Sara completely by surprise. Her throat dried. How could she tell him Steve thought Helen was dead? She steered round the subject lightly.

'You are right about the ghosts. On the first day I came to the château, I heard a sobbing noise in the upstairs passage.'

'I expect one of the maids had been reprimanded. It happens. Madame Darle is a wonderful housekeeper and very kind but there are times when she must be the strict disciplinarian.'

'With her son as well, I think.'

'Oh, yes. But you can take it from me they are very devoted. He may argue with her but he does not let anyone else say a word against her! As for my ghosts – they never sob. They only moan and float about the place waving their arms.' He regarded her solemnly through the yellow candlelight, a quirk on his lips.

She laughed.

Then, as if he had been waiting for her to drop her guard he repeated, 'Which ghost is Steve trying to contact, Sara?'

'Have you brought me all this way to ask me about Steve? How should I know what he is trying to do?'

'How indeed?'

'Or did you bring me along because you were afraid of returning to the château and finding one more ghost in your collection?'

'I like all my guests to see Paris. Before they return home,' he added quietly.

'Is . . . is that my dismissal notice? Is Mary coming back?' She tried to make her voice sound casual.

'Not yet – but I think you should consider returning to England – for your own safety. There have been too many accidents. And I have noticed an uneasiness in the village since you came.'

'Oh?' she said icily. 'You don't suppose it was there before, do you? Hidden beneath the surface?' She lifted the coffee cup to her lips. 'Or is it forbidden to make waves in Laffeine?'

They sat in silence, sipping coffee. It had a bitter taste to Sara.

'Why didn't you tell me there was a traitor in Laffeine during the war?' she asked at last.

'That was a rumour we buried with the corpses long ago.'

'Did you bury the traitor, too, or is he still in the village? If so, he must be afraid of me opening up the case of Sergeant John Parish. Afraid in case I find out something that will reveal his identity.'

'You know so little of war and what it means to be invaded,' Jules pointed out. 'Or of the suspicion and fear that drives ordinary people to behave in a way completely alien to them.'

'Are you condoning what happened?' she demanded.

'Of course not,' he answered angrily.

A waiter appeared from nowhere. 'More coffee, Monsieur?' Jules shook his head and tossed his napkin on to the table.

As Sara followed him from the room, she knew the evening was spoiled.

'I think I'll go to my room,' she said. The

tour round Paris and the wine that evening had combined to make her tired. In any case, there was no point in her and Jules spending any more time together.

He caught hold of her arm. 'It's foolish to spend the evening arguing. Especially in Paris. I want you to enjoy your visit.'

'Oh, I have, thank you,' she said stiffly.

As he escorted her to the staircase, they passed a room where there was a disco in progress. He smiled wryly.

'Keeping up with the times, I see.' Then to her utter and complete astonishment, he gripped her hand. 'You shall dance once in Paris,' he told her calmly.

She glanced towards the gyrating dancers. She couldn't imagine Jules indulging in such frenzied movements. But, before she could speak, he had pulled her with him under the swirling, coloured lights and was holding her close.

It was the wrong sort of dancing for a disco, but she knew by now Jules was a man who did as he pleased. The feel of his firm body against her own disturbed her greatly. Immediately, all her tiredness disappeared.

Chapter Sixteen

THEY walked together towards the Place de la Concorde after he suggested she might like some fresh air. The disco had become unbearably hot. He appeared to have forgotten that only a short time before they had been angry with one another and talked in an easy, pleasant manner as they strolled past boutiques and offices, and cafes with aromas of coffee and garlic wafting into the warm summer night.

'Years ago, this was a fashionable promenade for grand ladies in their carriages.'

As he related the history of the wide, busy street, she was gripped by a feeling of unreality. Was she, Sara Parish from Birmingham, really walking along the Champs-Élysées, under a sky peppered with stars with an attractive, sometimes awesome, Frenchman?

She assured herself it would have been as exciting had Matthew been at her side. But Matthew was in a different world. A million miles away.

Gazing at the brilliant, illuminated fountains, she sensed Jules studying her. She glanced at him. His expression did not change.

'You look very desirable tonight,' he said softly. She blushed.

Later, back at the hotel, he opened the door to her suite. He turned and looked down at her and touched her hair gently.

'You are sunshine and flames,' he whispered. After that, everything else in her world paled into nothing.

The next day he took her to the places he thought she would enjoy, including a cultural centre where jugglers and sword swallowers performed in the square outside, and she had her portrait drawn in charcoal. She was delighted with it.

'I shall become a brunette,' she declared.

'You shall not have the portrait unless you promise never to do such a thing,' he said teasingly. It caused a tremor inside her as she remembered what he had said the night before. And the look in his eyes.

The thought of leaving Laffeine made Sara feel empty. On the drive back to the château, she broached the subject again.

'Steve has told me about the fête you give every year when everyone from the village comes up to the château.'

'Ah, yes. We shall be having our summer fun day very soon.'

'Am I allowed to stay until then?' she asked quietly.

He did not answer. There was a bland expression on his face and she could not guess what he was thinking. 'I think it would be better for you if . . .'

'Please, Jules. I promise to be on my guard from now on. And I will leave straight after the fête.'

'And you will go back to England?'

'No.'

'What?'

'I shall find somewhere else to stay in Laffeine. I told you before, no one is going to drive me out. I shall go when I am ready.'

'I think you are the most obstinate woman I have ever met!'

'Don't be angry again.'

A smile touched the corners of his lips. 'Would you like me to stop the car and show you that I am not in the least angry?'

'No!' The word came out more sharply than she meant.

He glanced at her quickly.

After a moment, she said, 'Tell me about Helen.' She waited, half-fearful of his reaction. There was a long silence and just as she was thinking he had reverted into a sullen mood, he began to speak, softly at first.

'I met Helen when I was doing some research into the world of modelling for a suspense thriller. She was over here with a group from Britain. She was working for some mail order catalogue. I thought she was the most beautiful creature I had ever set eyes on.'

Sara only nodded.

'We had only been going together for a short time when she told me she was pregnant. More than anything I wanted to marry her. It was no problem as far as I was concerned.'

'During her pregnancy, she became restless and bored. I suggested a holiday and she went over to Scotland, but even after she returned and the baby was born, she could not seem to settle. I encouraged her to invite her friends over. She did. They came in their hordes.' He paused as he concentrated on the road ahead. The only sound was the purr of the engine.

Sara guessed it was difficult for him to talk about his wife and she made no comment. She was glad he was able to speak to her about Helen.

'It was my fault,' he continued. 'I should

have realised country living would be too dull for a girl like Helen, used to a more glamorous life. And it could not have helped much having a writer for a husband – always stuck in a study working. I expected too much.'

No, no, Sara wanted to cry. She had everything.

'Please – I shouldn't have asked you . . .' she began.

'Why not? Everyone must wonder why she left me. I do. God knows we had our differences, but I did not interfere with anything she wanted to do. With one exception . . .' He waved on a motorist itching to overtake a Rolls-Royce. 'She was well aware I would not tolerate any infidelity while she was married to me. Not after Michael was born.'

Sara glanced up curiously.

'You realise, of course, he is not my son?'

She stared. 'But he is just like you!'

'Maybe. But have you not noticed women fall for the same types over and over again?'

'Did . . .?' She stopped.

'Did I know when we married? Of course. But I was in love. And I love Michael. As far as I am concerned he is my son absolutely. My child!'

She noticed the muscles tauten in his brown arms as his hands gripped the driving wheel tightly. 'And no one is ever going to take Michael from me,' he added determinedly.

'Do you think Helen might try to do that?'

'She might. She left a note to say she would not be back – but Helen often said things she did not mean. And if, as I suspect, she has run away with Michael's father, there will come a time when they want the child.'

'Have you tried to find out who she went with?'

'Certainly not! When she walked out of my house, I washed my hands of her! She will never be allowed back there again.' He pressed his foot hard on the accelerator.

Sara was afraid of him in this mood. The night before had shown beyond all doubt that he could be tender and loving, but now he reminded her of someone in a Victorian melodrama. His views on women were unbending.

She did not condone what Helen had done, but neither could the woman be condemned out of hand because she had loved someone else outside her marriage. Not without even a hearing.

'Perhaps she's afraid to come back to Laffeine,' she said gently. 'After all, she must know as far as you are concerned she's behaved worse than any criminal. I don't suppose she dare look you in the face again.'

'And neither should she!'

'It can happen to anyone. None of us is perfect.'

'I had excused one indiscretion.'

'Oh, well – if you had excused her once.'

'Sarcasm does not become you.'

'Neither does taking on the role of God suit you.'

'She was my wife, Sara!' he shouted.

'She was a woman!' Sara retorted hotly, then she went cold. Whatever had possessed them both to refer to Helen in the past tense?

After that, her thoughts were in chaos. She recognised that he was high-handed and intolerant; that his views on women were old-fashioned, and yet despite all that, she could not understand Helen leaving him.

He had a magnetic attraction that could blind a woman to his faults; something about the expression in his clear, blue eyes that changed from brooding to sensual in a moment.

'Helen has a right to see Michael when she returns,' she said. 'She is his mother.'

'What sort of mother leaves her son for a year without trying to contact him? A year! A lifetime!'

Something about his tone made her heart sink. Did he still love Helen? she asked herself. She wished desperately she had not gone to Paris with him. For a little while, she had forgotten who he was. She had floated in a big bubble of fantasy. But bubbles always burst.

She had wanted to ask him about his own affairs. Or if the rules on infidelity only applied to women? Now it no longer mattered one way or the other.

She jumped as his fingers suddenly gripped hers. 'My wife ceased to exist for me when she left my house, Sara. As far as I'm concerned, Helen is dead.'

Chapter Seventeen

'PAPA!' They heard Michael screaming as they drove into the driveway. He stood on the château steps waving his arms. Tears were streaming down his cheeks.

Jules screeched the car to a stop, leaped out and swung the boy off his feet.

Sara saw him holding Michael close, wiping his eyes, coaxing him to be calm. She could not make out what Michael was saying through his sobs.

Suddenly, Jules thrust the child into her arms. 'Take care of him,' he ordered brusquely then ran two at a time up the steps and into the château.

Sara put her arms round the little boy. 'Darling! What is it?'

'Steve's dead!'

The blood drained from her face. She put her cold, trembling hand into Michael's and took him indoors.

Madame Darle was scurrying across the hall, her face pasty-grey.

'Madame! What has happened?'

The housekeeper's fists were clenched, her face drawn. 'Monsieur Steve was taken very ill,' she whispered.

'Is – is he . . .?'

'The doctor said it was food-poisoning, but he thinks he is over the worst.'

Sara breathed deeply, then she sank on to the nearest seat and drew Michael beside her. 'Steve is going to be all right, darling.

He's been ill, he isn't dead.'

His eyes were blue pools of fear. 'Crystal was crying.'

'I expect she was frightened.'

'I was frightened.'

'Of course you were.'

'Uncle Steve fell over at the picnic.' Michael shook his bright curls. 'He's dead!' he mimicked in a childish trill. 'They've done for him now!'

An icy chill ran up Sara's spine.

'What did you say?' she whispered.

He took a toy car from his pocket and started running it along the arms of the seat. She saw that already the incident was fading from his memory like a bad dream. She could ask him no more questions.

He zoomed the car at her and grinned. 'Vrrrooom!'

'I think it's time you were in bed,' she said, smiling at the little boy. 'Would you like me to read you a story?'

He nodded eagerly. Halfway up the stairs he asked, 'What's dead?'

After tucking Michael into bed, Sara went to the kitchen to find Crystal. Everything there was in chaos. Madame Darle had lost her calm, efficient manner and was scolding everyone in sight.

'It must have been the pies,' she was saying warningly. 'Everything else was prepared here.'

'Where did they come from, Madame?' Sara asked.

'From Monsieur Narbon, of course!' the older woman answered irritably. 'We always have his pies. They are excellent . . . Oh, no, it could not have been those.' She waved her arms at a maid carrying a jug of water. 'What have you got there, girl? Let me see it!'

Sara could not believe it was the same woman. The housekeeper was rushing to and fro like an animal in a trap. Suddenly she saw Pascal appear from a corner of the kitchen. He ambled across to his mother and murmured to her.

'What do you mean?' Madame shrieked. 'I have too much to do to—'

Pascal clamped his broad hands on her shoulders and pressed her down into a chair. 'Sit down, you will make yourself ill.'

'Go away!' She almost spat the words at him.

For a second, Sara thought she was going to hit or kick him.

He stood mutely, planted in front of her, making a wall with his thick, muscular

146

body. It was an odd relationship between the two of them; a mixture of fierce love and spitting hate so intermingled as to be unfathomable.

Gradually, Madame's eyes became less feverish. She shrugged. It was almost a gesture of hopelessness, Sara thought. Before leaving the kitchen, Pascal told one of the young maids to make his mother a cup of coffee. At the same time, he slid his hand down surreptitiously and squeezed the girl's buttocks hard.

She swung round to protest, but, as her eyes met his, she bit her lip and shrank away. His lips stretched into a surly grin. Then he picked up a huge basket of logs as easily as if it had been a box of matches.

Sara found Crystal at last. She was in her room kneeling on a single, sagging bed.

'Crystal! Are you all right?'

'*Mon Dieu*! Who would be a woman?'

'Is the baby coming?'

'How do I know? I have never had a baby before.'

'I'm going to get the doctor,' Sara said, turning towards the door.

'I do not want the doctor! And I do not want the baby!' The maid stretched her legs

147

slowly until she was sitting in an upright position. There was a combined smell of garlic and alcohol about her. Her hair tumbled in untidy strands across her face and her dress was dirty and taut across her stomach.

She rolled over awkwardly and grabbed at a cigarette packet. As she inhaled deeply, she glanced at Sara.

'Want one?'

'Why did you have the baby if you didn't want it?' Sara asked gently.

Crystal stared at her. 'Stay here long enough and you will find out for yourself,' she answered rudely.

'What does that mean?' Sara said sharply.

Crystal looked away. 'You have chanced your luck for too long,' she muttered. 'And do not tell me I should have had an abortion. My religion will not allow it.'

'What happened at the picnic, Crystal?'

Crystal puffed at her cigarette. 'I am not fit to talk. I am ill.'

'You are drunk!' Sara was rapidly losing patience with the girl.

The maid glared at her. 'You are made of ice!' Then tears welled in her eyes. 'We went for a picnic. After Steve had eaten, he collapsed.'

'Did you all eat the same food?'

Crystal sniffed. 'Michael had honey and banana sandwiches with raisins; I had ham and cheese. Steve had a pie – and caviare and crisp sandwiches.'

If it had not been so serious a topic, Sara would have grinned at the odd assortment of fillings.

'Do you think it was the pie?' she asked.

'I had pie, too.'

'Perhaps it was the caviare?'

'He had shrimps also.'

'No wonder he was sick.'

'He was not just sick. He was strange with it. He had hallucinations – and then he became unconscious.'

'Crystal, do you suppose someone could have tampered with his food?'

'No, no!' Crystal shook her head furiously. 'You see, he prepared it himself. We were all laughing. He was cutting the bread so badly no one could slice it properly afterwards.'

'And neither you nor Michael felt poorly after the picnic?'

'*Non.*'

'What was wrong with you when I came in here?'

Crystal pouted and patted her stomach. 'I

have the cramps – and look at my ankles. They swell . . . see? I am very delicate.'

'What did you do when Steve collapsed?'

'I screamed, of course.'

'Did you tell Michael Steve was dead?'

'*Oui*. I thought he was dead.'

'You frightened the boy!'

'How do you think I felt? That boy! He is driving me crazy. He is never still. Wanting this. Wanting that. He is a crazy child.' She stubbed out her cigarette viciously. 'He is so spoiled. I have had enough of . . .'

'Why did you yell out, "They have done for him?"'

Crystal stared at her. 'What are you talking about? If the boy told you that he is a liar! I am a sick woman. You have no right to come here questioning me – making up things about me.' Her voice rose in anger.

There was a loud rap at the door. Madame Darle stood in the open doorway, stony-faced. She ignored Sara and glanced at Crystal.

'If you are in labour, say so. If not, I need you in the kitchen.'

The two women argued rapidly in French. Then, Crystal rose sulkily, and combed her hair.

Sara was walking away when she heard her wail, 'I am having a baby!'

'So are millions of other women,' Madame retorted. 'In the war I had my baby behind a hedge.'

Sara was puzzled by Madame Darle's remark. She had understood from what she'd heard that Pascal had been born before the war started.

Chapter Eighteen

STEVE was moved to the local hospital where he recovered quickly.

Sara went to see him and found him still pale and weak.

'You're the one person I've been waiting to see,' he said, making it sound like a complaint. He was sitting on his bed wearing a dressing-gown.

'I'm flattered. Where shall I put these flowers?'

They went to sit in the day-room where streaming sunshine showed up his pallor even more. Sara settled herself in a basket chair opposite him. 'Do you think you

151

caught some sort of bug?'

'Like hell, I did. Somebody got at my food before we went on the picnic.'

'But you prepared it yourself.'

'And left it when I went to drag Michael out from the raspberry canes.'

'Oh, Steve . . . no one would poison you. Everybody adores you.'

'They all adore Jules, too. If anyone thought I was doing anything that might harm him, they wouldn't think twice about having a go at me.'

'Don't be silly. You wouldn't hurt Jules in any way. I know he irritates you, but . . .'

'Wouldn't I?'

She frowned. 'You aren't well, Steve . . .'

'If the police were given evidence which showed Helen did not intend leaving home, life might be damned awkward for Jules.'

She sighed. 'What are you trying to say?'

'I found her diary.'

'Where?'

'In their bedroom.'

'You . . . you went into their room while Jules was away? Whatever possessed you?' Sara was shocked at what he'd admitted, but curious, too.

'She did. Helen possessed me.'

152

Sara groaned.

Steve scowled. 'I know you don't believe in . . .'

'Spirit raising? No, I don't.'

'It works. I sat in the quiet and blanked my mind totally. I swung the pendulum. I was like an empty vessel waiting for free spirits to enter and take possession. And time and time again I got a picture of their bedroom in my mind – like television flashing off and on. So I went to their bedroom.

'For ages I couldn't see anything – and then it occurred to me to turn one of the big knobs on the bedstead. When it moved at last, I felt certain before I looked that there would be something in there. It was a small diary, rolled into the tube under the knob.'

'So you read it?'

'You bet your sweet life I did!'

'I think I had better be going . . .'

'Sara!' He caught hold of her hand. 'Someone knows I've got the diary. I heard them following me back to my room. My God, I couldn't get in there quickly enough. I even dropped the damned book at one point. They must have seen it. I believe that person tried to poison me – to stop me handing it over to the police and implicating Jules in a sticky situation.'

He gave a grim laugh. 'It's the last thing on my mind, giving it to them.' He took a book from his pocket and smoothed out one of the pages. 'Listen. *Michael to dentist tomorrow. Poor baby. Lots of treats after.*' He looked up. 'She was whacky about Michael. Always took him to the doctor and dentist herself. No way would she have left someone else to spoil him with cake and cookies. His treat would be her treat. Does that sound like a mother about to take off for a year?'

'Well, it's hard to make it tally with the letter Jules says she left him.'

Sara wished with all her heart she could wash her hands of the whole sordid business.

'One thing is certain,' she said miserably. 'You have to give that diary to the police.'

'Never!'

'What do you mean?'

'It's all so ironical. I could have saved the would-be poisoner such a lot of bother. The diary has reinforced all my suspicions – but I can't show it to anyone. Except you, of course. But then I trust you to say nothing to anyone.'

'You mean – you won't implicate Jules after all?'

'I don't give a damn about Jules. But I can't implicate Helen.' He threw the little book on her lap. 'Read it.'

Chapter Nineteen

SARA frowned as she fingered the small, brown book. It seemed awful to her to delve into another woman's private world.

Steve watched as she hesitated, then he leaned forward and snatched the diary from her. 'For heaven's sake, Sara! It isn't easy for me, either. I'm not peeling away the layers of Helen's life out of morbid curiosity. It is something I have to do. I intend to find out if Jules did anything to harm Helen – and, by God, if he did . . .'

'Aren't you just a bit obsessed with Jules and what you think he did?'

'Funny for you to make such a remark. Ever since you came back from Paris I've had the feeling you are somewhat obsessed with him yourself!'

'That is absolute nonsense!' Her cheeks were burning.

'Yes, it is, he's too old for you.'

Sara bit back her reply. After a few moments, she said as calmly as she could, 'We aren't discussing me. We're discussing your aunt and her husband.'

Steve leaned back in the basket chair and folded his arms. 'Jules has everything off a little too pat for my liking – that neat little typewritten note to prove she was intending to leave him . . .'

'I know, you've told me . . . and he forged her signature. It's all pure surmise, Steve,' Sara protested.

'What about the quarrel they had on the night she left? I heard them and so, probably, did most of the staff. It was obvious to everybody they weren't getting on any more.'

'That is even more reason for her to leave him,' she pointed out.

'Never! Helen would never go away from the château of her own free will.'

His vehemence caused her to look at him quickly. 'But if she had fallen in love with . . .' she began.

'She was already in love. With money. With everything it could give her – and that isn't the derogatory statement it sounds.'

'Oh?'

He inhaled deeply. 'My Aunt Helen had a

miserable, deprived childhood. She told me all about it. So who's to blame her for making the most of her new-found wealth? And one thing is certain – when she did have plenty – she was damned generous. I owe her a lot. She made sure I wanted for nothing at college. No, she would never have left—'

'The goose that laid the golden eggs?'

'I told you – that's not the way it was! She loved Jules when they married. Perhaps if he hadn't left her alone so much–' He slumped back in his chair, staring at the floor. All the recent energy seemed to have left him and he looked depressed.

'What is it, Steve?' Sara asked gently.

After a few minutes of silence, he spoke. 'She was sleeping around with other men.'

Sara gazed at him in disbelief. 'Are you sure?' she whispered.

'Am I sure? Oh, God, I wish I wasn't.' He nodded towards the diary. 'It's all there – names, telephone numbers, and the dates she was going to meet them. Even some blokes from the village.' He gave a mirthless laugh. 'So you see, no one need have worried that I might give this to the police. Our family may not boast a long list of distinguished ancestors, but we do have our pride.'

Sara realised what it had cost Steve to tell her about Helen. He might have acted like a free-thinking student when he invited her into his bed, but it was obvious his aunt's promiscuity had shocked him deeply.

She suddenly felt very sorry for him, as he sat in the day-room. There was a look of defeat about him. The strong sunlight shining through the window showed up his extreme paleness.

'Do you suppose Jules knows about Helen?' she asked, horrified at the idea.

'I don't know – but somebody certainly wanted to silence me.'

Suddenly, their eyes met.

'I suppose you – er – can't vouch for Jules on the night you both spent in Paris together?' he said.

'No, I can't!' She jumped up from her chair.

He held up his hands in a gesture of mock terror. 'Sorry. Sorry. But he does have a way with women, and I don't suppose you would be the—'

'I have to go,' she interrupted him coldly.

'Oh, Sara, don't be like that. Come back. I need your help.'

As she was walking away, Sara saw that

an old lady in a wheelchair, who had been regarding them curiously from the other side of the room, now smiled thinly and waved a bony hand at Steve.

He turned from following Sara and went to speak to her. When he left her, the old lady was chuckling happily.

Sara had watched this and now, her anger gone, she walked back towards him. Steve had a charm of his own and it was difficult to remain at odds with him.

'What help do you want from me, Steve?'

He smiled up at her. 'I want you to put the diary back.'

Sara could hardly believe her ears. 'You have to be joking? You actually want me to go sneaking into Jules' room, like you did?'

'You are the only person I can trust. I have to get rid of the blasted book. It's like a weight round my neck, I wish I'd never seen it.'

'So much for the runes,' Sara muttered.

'Well, at least it's shown us that if Jules knew about Helen's activities he had a motive for getting rid of her. He's got this thing about loyalty in his women.'

It was the first time he had made such a blatant accusation outright.

She rounded on him, her anger returning

in force. 'That is a terrible thing to say and you know it! OK – so you had a lot to thank your aunt for, but don't you realise it all came indirectly from Jules? And I expect it came with his blessing, too. He is one of the most generous—'

She stopped, her cheeks flushed.

Steve was gazing at her curiously.

She lowered her voice. 'You have reason to be grateful to both of them.'

'And have you a reason for wanting to protect Jules, Sara?'

Sara felt a dull ache inside as she drove back to the château. She hardly noticed the lush Burgundy valleys and the wide, winding river flowing like a lazy snake.

Her thoughts were on Jules. She ought to hand the diary over to someone in authority. But they would probably put the same interpretation on it as Steve had done.

They might believe that Jules had found out about Helen's affairs and had been angry enough to kill her.

Sara shuddered. She was getting far too involved with matters that were none of her concern. She was sorry she had allowed Steve to persuade her to help him.

That night, she undressed and sat reading

in her room until the château was absolutely silent. She had seen a light in Jules' study and knew that he was working late as usual.

She put on a silky housecoat and padded along the corridors to his bedroom. When she reached it, she was overcome with guilt and nearly turned back. She found the whole situation distasteful.

The big, oak door creaked ominously and her heart thudded. Then she stepped quickly into the room and switched on the light.

It could only have been Jules' room. It was superb. Oak-panelled and with an ornate ceiling that made her gasp. It was divided into octagonal shapes with exquisite paintings in each section.

She moved quickly past the walnut writing-desk and the Hepplewhite love seat to the bed. She tried to turn one of the brass bedknobs, but it would not move. Her hands were damp now with perspiration. She wiped them on her housecoat and tried again, but still she couldn't budge it.

Panic swept over her. She kneeled on the bed to tackle the second knob from a different angle. As the bedroom door opened, she sank back on to her heels and stared towards it, petrified.

'Sara!' There was astonishment registered in Jules' blue eyes. 'I thought I heard some-one in here, but I never expected to find . . .' He closed the door softly behind him, his gaze fixed on her all the time. 'I'm glad you came.' His voice was deep and the sound of it made her tremble.

She felt herself unable to move or speak. She stared, half-mesmerised, as he approached the bed, his hands outstretched towards her. It was only the movement of the bed as he sat beside her that brought her to her senses.

She slid away from him. 'I – I didn't–' she began.

'It is not necessary to explain. Not in my country,' he murmured. He drew closer to her and enclosed her arms with his fingers.

'You don't understand!' she exclaimed. But he silenced her with his mouth. There was a screaming inside her but she could not move. Then she felt a sensation of floating on silk sheets. As he kissed her she became aware of his mounting emotions and intimate caresses.

Jules had no inhibitions whatsoever.

'No!' she cried at last. 'This is not what you think . . .'

'Why do we spoil it by thinking?' he

whispered.

'Because you are married. That's why!' She blinked back her tears and sat up.

His hands seized hers. 'I have told you – as far as I am concerned, Helen is dead!'

'Don't keep saying that.'

'Listen, Sara,' he said, pulling her close again, 'she left me of her own accord. Long before she went she made it very clear that she had become tired of my company. So much so, I stayed out of her way as much as possible." His eyes glinted like steel. 'It was not because of choice I spent all my time shut in my study.' He shook his head. 'I am not an idiot. I know she wanted more from life than she found with me.'

'What do you mean?' She thought about the diary still in her pocket.

'It does not matter – anyway, she will not be my wife for much longer.'

'Why not?'

'I have begun divorce proceedings. I should have done so before this, but in my family divorce has never been the way of things. However – times have changed.' He frowned. 'Just as Helen and I changed. Our marriage was in name only long before she left me. So, you see, Sara, there is no need for all this guilt on your part—'

163

'I should not have come here. It was a dreadful mistake. I – I must go, Jules.'

'Sara!'

'Good night.'

He reached the door before she did, standing with his back to it, the broad expanse of his shoulders making a formidable barrier against her.

'Let me out, please?' she asked, her voice shaking a little.

But his expression darkened by the minute. 'Forgive me for my stupidity,' he said sarcastically. 'But I find it somewhat perplexing that you should come to my bedroom at all. You knew very well what would happen.'

'No, I . . . Oh, Jules, I know this all looks very odd,' she said miserably.

'Odd? No – that is not the word I would choose for a woman who deliberately sets out to provoke a man, then–'

'It wasn't that way at all.'

'Then how would you describe it?' He gripped her shoulders, making her wince.

'Let me go! You're hurting me.'

His face was close to hers and she could see the anger in his eyes. He stared at her for a moment longer, then slowly his fingers slackened. He opened the door.

'I suggest you don't make a habit of this,' he said icily. 'Unless you are prepared for the consequences.'

She dragged her feet back to her room, wondering how she could have been so stupid. She hated Jules. But most of all she hated herself for not having the courage to tell him about the diary and finding out if he knew of Helen's affairs.

She rolled on top of her bed in the oppressive heat of the summer night. Would she ever be able to sleep again? She tingled with a thousand sensations. The pillows were silken-soft against her naked flesh, like those on the bed where Jules lay. She shivered. She had been crazy to take such a risk. She had known he might walk in at any minute.

Chapter Twenty

SARA gazed from her window as the sun shone brightly on the morning of the fête. It was like looking at eternity stretching out before her through the rich, green country-side to the shimmering, blue sky beyond.

She had loved the view but now it only acted as a reminder that it would be there for ever, to charm and dazzle the next occupant of the room, whereas she would soon be leaving.

During the morning there was chaos as the gardens were transformed – everyone was frantically busy. Servants carried glasses and sparkling red and white wines to the tables erected on the lawn. Cheeses, salads and cakes waited in disorganised array on the terrace.

Villagers, who had been helping since dawn, were roping off sections of the grass to be used for stalls and side-shows. Others staggered along under the weight of straw bales that would act as seats or barriers. Balloons and orange and red lanterns were being positioned in the trees ready for the evening's dancing.

Sara was carrying crockery to the barbecue area when she saw Michael running behind Madame Darle, his eyes shining and never for a minute shifting from the dish of ripe fruit he held. Suddenly, two peaches fell and rolled across the terrace.

Madame swung round, '*Mon Dieu*! Didn't I tell you to leave that for me?' She snatched the dish from him.

166

Sara was staggered. She had never seen her behave so impatiently. But then, since Steve's mysterious illness she had not been herself.

The corners of Michael's lips drooped and his chin quivered.

Pascal saw him and laid down the trestle table he was carrying. He strode over to the little boy and swung him up on to his shoulders. Then he started galloping round the lawn. Michael clung to Pascal's chin and began to laugh. Everyone joined in, including Sara. But she saw that Madame had rushed indoors.

'Isn't your mother very well?' she asked Pascal when he came back with Michael.

'Today is very busy for her and she has a lot to think about, that is all, Mademoiselle. The fête is very special. She wishes it to be perfect, of course. It is good you will see it before you leave.'

He had never spoken to her so pleasantly. But how did he know she had finally decided to leave? Certainly, she had phoned Matthew to tell him she was coming home and there was always the chance someone had overheard her.

The night after Jules had caught her in his room, Sara had stayed awake long into the night, reasoning with herself that it was pointless to stay any longer in France. She would leave her grandfather to rest in peace even if it did mean giving in to the person who was trying to frighten her off. In a few days, she doubted if Jules would even remember her.

Pascal was actually smiling at her now. His huge, hairy arms lifted Michael down. He adjusted the enormous buckle on his belt.

'There will be dancing tonight. You like to dance?'

'Yes, I do.'

'Me, also.' He ambled away. She saw him bend his massive body to pick up the table again. Then he turned with it, and looked towards Sara. It reminded her of the first day she had come to the château. How his eyes had devoured her.

She turned quickly to Michael. 'Come along – we'll go for a walk.'

He clung to her hand as they made their way towards the lake.

'Are you going away, Sara?'

'Yes, I am, Michael. You knew I was only here for a short time, didn't you?'

'Who's going to look after me?'

'Why, Crystal will.'

'Crystal smacks me.'

Sara frowned. 'All little boys get a smack sooner or later,' she said more lightly than she felt.

'Mary didn't smack me.'

'Mary was a saint, that's why!' She grinned at him.

Half-understanding, he burst into childish giggles and suddenly raced away from her. She ran after him.

'Michael! Come back!'

'Catch me. Catch me.' He tore in and out of the trees. Sara flew into the wood and saw him leaping up and down on a small, wooden jetty at the edge of the lake. He was clapping his hands and yelling, 'Papa!'

Jules was speeding across the water in a sleek metal-blue speed-boat. He headed towards them and cut the engine, gliding into the jetty where Sara was standing breathless and dishevelled, gripping hold of Michael.

Jules stretched out a lean, brown arm to catch hold of one of the jetty posts. He balanced himself, frowning at Sara. He looked fit and bronzed.

'He shouldn't be alone on this jetty. This is a deep stretch of water with a lot of weed in it.'

'Yes—' she began, but Jules was glaring at his son.

'I've told you before.'

'But Sara wanted a ride in the boat, Papa.'

Sara felt the colour stream into her cheeks. There was a hint of amusement in Jules' face.

'Who wants a ride, Mike?'

'Me, I do,' Michael whispered.

'OK then – but no coming down to this jetty on your own again.' Jules lifted the lid of one of the seats in the boat and brought out a life-jacket.

After Sara had helped Michael put it on, Jules threw one to her.

'I was helping with the fête . . .' she began.

'I'd like you to take Michael back with you after his ride so you may as well come, too.'

Sitting beside Michael, she could sense how excited the little boy was. She held his hand reassuringly as the boat surged out across the lake again. But soon they were racing at a speed that took her breath away.

'Don't be frightened, Sara,' Michael said, laughing excitedly.

She laughed. She had never felt so

exhilarated. Spray splattered her cheeks. Her hair blew in the wind. She was almost sorry when Jules cut the engine and allowed the boat to drift.

'Can I do the anchor?' Michael pleaded.

'Not today, Mike. We have to go back shortly.'

'Can't we even fish?'

'This is not our day to fish, is it?' He glanced at Sara. 'Every year on fête day I like to make sure myself that all my boats are in top-class condition. It is traditional for men from the village to take them out and fish as long as they like.' He was speaking to her as if she were a stranger being taken on a tour of the grounds.

'It is very beautiful out here,' she murmured. It was true and she meant it. The wide lake was like a shiny plate with willows dipping leisurely fingers from the banks.

'There is no peace like that of drifting on water. Alone,' he added.

After that, she was silent. Her appearance in his bedroom for all the wrong reasons obviously still rankled with him. The only sound came from water gently lapping at the boat.

Michael shouted his impatience to be off and Jules started up the engine again.

By late afternoon, there were visitors thronging the grounds of the château.

Sara recognised some of the faces.

'Where do you suppose all this lot sneaked in from?' a voice asked behind her.

'Steve!' Sara swung round. She was delighted to see him back at the château again and, with an involuntary movement, she flung her arms about him.

To her astonishment, he reciprocated by pulling her to him and kissing her. As he relaxed his grip, she saw Jules appear from the crowd.

He walked solemnly towards them.

'Hello, Steve. Welcome home,' he said quietly.

'Jules.' Steve only nodded briefly.

'It's good to see you looking so much better than you did in hospital.'

'Thanks.'

Jules glanced at Sara then Steve. 'Enjoy yourselves, both of you. And, please, help yourselves to the food.'

After he had gone, Steve muttered, 'Only if he tastes it first.' He turned to Sara. 'Did you put it back?'

'If you mean the diary – no, I didn't. Jules—'

'Where is it now?' he interrupted,

frowning.

'Don't worry. It's safe. Locked in my week-end case. Nobody will tamper with that.'

'Oh, my God! You are too trusting by far. I don't trust anyone.'

She followed his gaze to where Jules was talking to Matilde in the shady seclusion of a tree. Matilde was laughing coquettishly and tapping his arm. Jules was smiling his lazy intimate smile at her.

Sara was startled by the pang she felt inside. 'Come on, Steve,' she said, a little too sharply. 'This is supposed to be a fun day. Let's have fun.'

'Where do we go to have it?' he asked mischievously.

'We go to where they are bowling for a pig,' she replied dryly.

He laughed. 'You know what? You look really good today. I like you in that white dress. You have a fabulous figure,' he added admiringly.

Sara had never seen so much food. Tables were top-heavy with rich, cold meats, elaborate salads, freshly-baked bread, Brie and Camembert cheeses, with black, green, and pickled olives. There were tiered cake stands showing off exotic gateaux and home-made tarts full of dairy cream. She saw tubs of ice-cream in all colours and flavours, and baskets of ripe fruit.

Sara and Steve carried their plates of food to the terrace and sat under a gaily-striped umbrella near the foliage-covered trellis. Fat sprays of greenery burst out from ornamental pots on the pink tiles. She looked at the crowds in their dazzling summer clothes and tried to absorb the scene. She wanted to remember it always.

'Are all these people from the village, Steve?'

'Most of them. But some are Jules' friends and I expect there are plenty who knew Helen.'

At that moment he saw someone Helen had known and excused himself to speak to her.

Sara watched him as he hurried towards the woman. He would not be happy until he had unearthed everything anyone knew about his aunt. She admired his tenacity and sense of duty, but wondered when he would get on with living his own life instead of becoming obsessed with runes and pendulums – and the past. But then, hadn't she been obsessed with the past?

It was strange to think that soon she

174

would be on her way to Calais with this, like all holidays, becoming a hazy memory. She would doubtless forget Steve and Jules . . . then Sara admitted honestly to herself that this would probably prove impossible.

Suddenly she saw Crystal. She was rushing across the lawn between groups of people. She looked as if she had come from the wood. She had a strained, distressed expression. Sara looked round quickly for Michael and to her relief saw him playing with some other children. She followed Crystal to see if she needed help. Her baby was due any day.

After all the chattering and laughing outside, the château felt hollow and empty. Sara's light, summer sandals echoed on the flagstones.

'Crystal, what is it?' she cried when she found the maid sobbing in one of the pantries.

'I hate him. I hate all men!'

'Who do you hate?'

'He does not know the meaning of love. He does not even know I exist.'

'Who? The father of your child?'

'No man wants me like this, I am gross.'

'Oh, no, that isn't true—'

'But he wanted me enough to make me lie

with him, didn't he? On that foggy night in the woods. Oh, yes, that was different.' She jabbed her finger at her stomach. 'Now he should marry me.'

Tears coursed down her cheeks. 'He is with another woman. I have just seen them together. Then after her there will be another – and another—'

'And you want to marry a man like this?'

'He will give my baby a name!' Suddenly, her eyes were blazing. She grabbed at Sara's hands. 'But he will not get away with it. I know plenty about him. Oh, yes, I could tell you something—'

A door banged. Both women froze. Crystal's jaw dropped open. After a moment, she turned and whispered to Sara, 'I cannot tell you now. It isn't safe. Anyone could come in. But I will tell you before you go. You will see.' She wiped at her eyes vigorously and left Sara on her own.

Chapter Twenty-One

THAT evening there was dancing on the lawns under brightly-glowing lanterns. The band played its own French brand of country music. Couples danced on the grass and the terraces.

Suddenly, Sara felt alone among the festivity. Michael was in bed, Jules was mingling with his guests, and Steve was dancing with a pretty girl from the village.

She wandered across to the lake. It was adorned with lights from the sterns of the boats where people were fishing. On her way back to the dancing, she heard a rustle in the bushes near her. Then a low groan. On looking closer she saw Alain Narbon, the handsome, young son of Laffeine's butcher. He was with one of the maids. Sara turned quickly and hurried away, her cheeks hot.

'Mademoiselle!'

To Sara's consternation, she saw Alain's parents coming through the wood towards her. She stammered a greeting and was about to leave them when Pierre put out his hand.

'Please – we must speak to you.'

'We are so ashamed,' his wife murmured. 'But we cannot speak to you where we will be seen.'

'Then come this way, Madame, where it is more secluded.' Sara led them farther away from where their son was lying.

'Please call me Claudette – I think we have been very rude to you. We did not keep our promise to invite you to our home.'

'But it doesn't matter,' Sara began.

'It matters very much!' Pierre exclaimed. 'We are not people who go back on our word – but after you had come to the shop someone threw a brick through our window with a note tied to it warning us to keep silent about your grandfather.'

'Keep silent indeed,' Claudette said bitterly. 'What on earth did we have to say to anyone? We only knew the same as everyone else – that a traitor in the village had betrayed the soldier – but no one knew who it was. Or if that person were alive or dead. We told everyone about the note and that we would not be intimidated.'

'But then dreadful things started to happen to us,' Pierre said. He shrugged. 'And you see – my old mother, she lives with us . . .'

Sara felt sorry for them both. 'Monsieur Gouvan told me about the incident with the chickens,' she said.

'Ah – he alone was not afraid to talk to you. He puts all of us to shame.' Pierre glanced round furtively. 'Some of us have been to his house for a meeting. There were others who had threatening letters, too, but now we are united. We shall no longer be intimidated.' His eyes glittered in the half-light.

'What have you done?' Sara felt uneasy. Her presence had caused enough trouble. What was going to happen now?

Pierre lowered his voice. 'In the war there was one German soldier who was not like the others. He was kind, talked to us as if we were human beings. We learned to respect him. Sadly, he died, but after the war his son came to see us. He was a nice boy—'

'Until she gobbled him up,' Claudette interrupted.

'Sshh!' Pierre frowned heavily.

'Why should we hide it? Haven't we hidden enough?' Claudette narrowed her eyes and looked at Sara. 'She brought dishonour to the name of "Clare"!'

'Claudette!' Pierre spoke sharply.

'She would have had all of you if she could. But she did not have my Pierre,' his wife finished triumphantly.

'You are a silly, old woman,' her husband whispered, but the anger had left his voice.

How many lives had Helen upset? Sara thought. She prayed Jules never knew how many. 'And the soldier's son?' she asked. 'Did you talk to him about what happened in the war?'

Pierre shook his head. 'Very little. It was not encouraged. It was – how do you say? – uncomfortable for all of us. We had become friends.'

'But now we have written to him,' Claudette informed her.

Sara looked from one to the other.

'Since you came here, Mademoiselle Sara, we have been reliving our guilt. We can't bury our heads any longer and pretend it never happened,' Pierre said. 'The time has now come for all niceties to be swept away and to dig for the truth. And that is what we are doing.

'We have asked Klaus if his father ever spoke about the person in Laffeine who was helping the Gestapo. We have told him what has been happening here. And, Mademoiselle, he is coming to see us. You must come to meet him.'

'But I am leaving—'

'No, no. This is important for all of us. Do you not want to know who betrayed your grandfather? You see – he knows. He knows!'

Sara felt a tide of emotions sweep over her. How could she tell them it no longer mattered to her? Nothing could alter the past. Life had to go on. Bitterness and brooding only brought unhappiness. She had seen that.

What did matter, was that she had stirred up something evil that was festering in Laffeine. Could she now turn her back and walk away, leaving others to face the consequences?

'What will happen when you discover the traitor's identity, Pierre?' she asked.

He shrugged. 'Leave that to us.'

'You will inform the police?'

'Of course.'

She breathed a sigh of relief. Then she caught her breath again as Pierre continued.

'Why should we not? After all, Jacques, the policeman who lives in Laffeine, is the son of one who was also betrayed. He knows already what we shall do.'

'Pierre,' Sara said anxiously, 'the war has been over for years. If you go taking matters into your own hands—'

'Justice shall be meted out according to the crime,' he said simply.

Claudette slipped her hand into his and

nodded.

The glow of the moon through the trees gave their faces an eerie silver sheen. It lit up hollows under their eyes.

'And this time,' Pierre went on in a flat voice, 'it will be us who decide the manner of death.'

Sara stared at them both. She could not be hearing them properly. This was the twentieth century. They were not in a time when mobs took the law into their own hands.

Or were they?

'Don't worry, *ma petite*,' Claudette said, patting Sara's arm. 'Your grandfather's death shall be avenged. We promise.'

'But—' Sara began.

'Alain!' Pierre shouted suddenly.

Sara turned to see two figures running from behind a bush in the distance.

'Who is the girl?' Pierre demanded of his wife. 'Always another girl!' He put out his arm. 'Come, we shall find out.' He turned to Sara. 'My house – tomorrow at three. Please come.'

Sara gazed after them. She knew without being told that their revenge when it came would be worse than anything the traitor could expect from the law.

They might have buried their memories but they would never forget. Members of the Maquis who had been betrayed had been their friends. She had heard terrible stories. Steve had told her of prisoners who had been hung by their ankles and left to die. And much worse.

She shivered.

When she reached the terrace again the music was still blaring out. She wondered at the stamina of the villagers. Faces were flushed and excited. There were even some children still running about.

There was a change of tempo and the band played a sleepy waltz. The older women beamed.

'Are you all right, Sara?' She was surprised to see Jules regarding her closely, his eyes darkly blue in the moonlight.

'Fine,' she replied brightly.

He took her by the hand to join the dancing. Had he forgotten their confrontation? He drew her close. Her heart beat faster, but under his firm direction, she followed easily and without faltering.

'Are you going to tell me why you came to my room?' he murmured.

She swallowed. 'I . . . I can't. But it was

not what you thought.'

'Pity,' he said softly.

She flushed and drew away from his tight hold.

Then he began to talk with the pleasant politeness that she hated. 'So – what are you intending to do when you get back home? Teaching again?'

She nodded. 'I shall be very busy. I'm going to be deputy head of a department.'

'You are ambitious?'

As she talked to him of plans formulated before she left Birmingham she thought how unreal it all sounded. Reality was the Château du Bois; Laffeine, where her grandfather was buried.

She wondered fleetingly if she was leaving because she was a coward. Not that she was afraid because attempts had been made on her life – that only served to infuriate her and make her more determined than ever to discover the truth about the past. But there was a deeper fear, a tangled emotion inside her.

'I expect I shall see you before you go,' Jules was saying. 'If not, I hope you have a pleasant journey.'

'Thank you,' she whispered.

'And don't pick up any more hitch-hikers!'

His eyes met hers. All levity vanished from his expression. In that one moment, they both understood why she was leaving. She felt his hands tighten their grip on her. Round them, people were dancing and laughing. The band blared out raucous "oom-pa-pa" noises. Balloons popped. Coloured paper streamers floated over them like confetti.

'Sara,' he said hoarsely.

She melted against him. She knew she would do whatever he wanted of her.

'Monsieur!'

The cry came from Pierre Narbon. He had forced his way through the crowd and stood beside Jules, ashen-faced and breathless.

'Come quickly, Monsieur. A body has been found in the lake.'

Chapter Twenty-Two

'JACQUELINE – would you please make coffee for everyone?' Sara asked, as the maid hurried past her.

'But, M'moiselle, I cannot find Madame anywhere, and . . .'

'I will take the responsibility, then,' Sara said. 'I should like you to take some to Monsieur Clare straight away, then to the police inspector and his assistant in the study.'

'But, Madame . . .'

'Now, please, Jacqueline,' Sara said firmly.

It was the early hours of the morning and extremely cold in the château in spite of the day having been so hot. The staff looked pale and shocked and were either sitting about listlessly waiting for their turn to be interviewed or standing together, whispering occasionally.

Sara had been to her room and changed into a light sweater and skirt.

The police had been on the scene very quickly after Helen's body had been dragged up from the thick, black silt at the bottom of the lake. An anchor from one of the fishing boats had caught on it. The man in the boat had thought the body was a bundle of old rags. It was identified in the first instance by a ring on one of the fingers that still had some flesh on it.

When Sara thought about it she closed

186

her eyes in horror. Poor Jules, she thought.

She saw his study door open. He stood in the entrance with the police inspector for a moment, then the sergeant was escorting him to the drawing-room, his hand lightly on Jules' back almost as if he was supporting him. She saw Steve leave the room then with the policeman and follow him to the study. She hurried across the hall.

Jules was hunched in an armchair, his head buried in his hands. Her heart ached for him. She wanted to reach out and touch him. To help him in some way. Sara sat quietly in another chair. He glanced up. His eyes were sunk into grey hollows. Lines etched round his mouth made him look older. Her eyes blurred suddenly.

'She – she had been stabbed.' He choked out the words. 'It was not an accident. She did not fall in the lake and drown. She was stabbed with a kitchen knife. It was still – it was still—' He could not go on.

'Hush,' she whispered, appalled by what he had said. For Helen to have drowned would have been terrible enough, but this! She stretched out her hand to him as he bent his head again, but drew it back without touching him. He was alone in his distress. She could not intrude.

A few minutes later, Jules sat up in the chair and took a deep breath. Getting up quickly, he marched over to the drinks cabinet. He poured himself a large brandy and tossed it down his throat.

'I have sent for some coffee,' Sara said hesitantly.

'The cure for all ills, even murder?' he asked cynically, and put down the glass with a thump. 'You know they think I did it?' he said dully.

'Oh, no, Jules—'

'Oh, yes, Jules. The trouble is, I can't pretend. I wish I could have stood in front of that sharp-eyed man in my study and told him I still loved Helen, even though she was involved with another man. That the weeks before she left weren't hell.' He took another deep breath and stared into space. 'It would have helped if I could have pretended to be racked with grief – instead of guilt.'

'Guilt?'

'If it had not been for me she might have been alive now.'

'What on earth are you talking about?'

'I could have spent more time with her. Seen the sort of people she went around with. Mixed with them. Made more of an effort to save our marriage.'

'It takes two—'

'I knew the sort of life she was used to when I married her.'

'You've got to stop blaming yourself for everything.'

'I am to blame,' he said harshly. 'If—'

'If, if, if!' she shouted. They stared at one another. She caught her breath. 'I'm sorry,' she said more quietly. 'But, you see, I know how you are feeling. When my mother died, everyone thought I was going to have a nervous breakdown. That's why I came on holiday.

'Although I had done everything I could for her while she was alive, afterwards I could only think of the times I had neglected her, been irritable or selfish. I really tortured myself – as if somehow I had to suffer, too. I was so eaten up with guilt, I was ill. So will you be if you go on like this.'

'Our cases aren't quite the same,' he retorted. He picked up the brandy decanter.

Sara put her hand over his as he was about to pour another drink.

'Did you know about the other men?' she asked softly.

'What are you talking about?'

'Helen left a diary. Before you load

yourself with any more guilt, I suggest you read it.'

There was a knock and Jacqueline came in with a tray of coffee and biscuits. She turned shyly to face Jules and spoke to him in rapid French.

His expression softened. 'Please tell all the staff I am grateful for their kind thoughts – and their sympathy.'

The maid dabbed at her eyes, sniffed, then hurried out.

When Jules looked at Sara again the gentleness had left his eyes. 'Perhaps you will get me this diary you spoke of.'

'Yes, of course . . .' She rose from her chair with flushed cheeks.

'Oh, Sara!' He strode across and took her in his arms.

She pulled away from him. 'I'll go and get the diary, Jules,' she said softly.

She hurried from the room. He was driving himself insane believing the break-up of the marriage had been all his fault. She could not watch his agony. He had to know the whole truth about Helen.

'Excuse me, Mademoiselle,' a voice said behind her when she reached the hall. 'The inspector would like a word with you, please.'

Sara followed the policeman to the study. She saw Steve come out, but he did not so much as glance at her. His face was white.

'So, you are on holiday here?' the inspector asked, smiling at her from astute grey-green eyes under bushy eyebrows. He was tall and thin, and sucked on a pipe. 'But it has been a stressful holiday, no?'

'I – I suppose it has.'

'Of course it has. Monsieur Clare has told us all about your "accidents." He seems very concerned for your safety. It would have been better had you come straight to us and told us about them.'

'But they were—'

'Instead of Monsieur Clare taking on the role of detective and spending so much time trying to solve the mysteries on his own,' he added, interrupting her.

'I did not realise he had been doing so,' Sara said in surprise.

'Being an eminent crime writer does not automatically give him the powers of the police.' The inspector tapped his empty pipe on the back of his hand and grinned. 'I expect we shall see a book out of this, M'moiselle. Although I would say that a snake hidden away in a car was a . . . a little too far-fetched, no?'

Sara frowned and felt uncomfortable. What was he getting at?

He scratched the back of his head and seemed to be concentrating deeply. 'I suppose it might happen if—'

'You don't believe me, do you?' Her eyes flashed.

'Monsieur Clare believed you – enough to question all his servants in turn, and visit some poachers in the village. He has been very busy on your behalf.'

Sara was staggered. She had not thought Jules had taken the incidents so seriously; in fact, there were times when he, too, seemed to think she had been exaggerating.

'So who am I not to listen with the same concern?' the inspector continued.

But by now Sara did not trust him one bit. Neither did she understand his line of questioning. He started to tap his teeth rhythmically with the stem of his pipe. It unnerved her. She felt like some sort of criminal under close scrutiny.

'You will have much to tell when you get home, will you not?' he said. 'Such exciting events to happen to an attractive young lady—'

'No, Inspector, not exciting,' she contradicted him coldly.

'Oh, come. A week-end in Paris with your attractive host? A man who rushes about for you trying to find out—'

'I know what you are suggesting!' Sara cried, jumping to her feet. 'That I made everything up to gain his attention. What sort of a woman do you think I am, Inspector? All right, so I find Monsieur Clare attractive. Most women would, and I am no exception. But neither am I an exhibitionist nor a liar. I do not need to resort to fairy stories to attract a man!'

'Sit down, M'moiselle.' He spoke quietly, but with authority.

Sara swallowed and did as he said. He came round, sat on Jules' desk and leaned towards her. 'You must understand, we have to find out the absolute truth from everyone.'

Only then did Sara fully understand. He had been testing her to find out if attempts on her life really had taken place or if she was a starry-eyed female looking for attention.

'I don't much like your methods, Inspector,' she said icily.

'It was necessary, Mademoiselle.' He was gentle now.

'And what has all this got to do with Madame Clare?'

'Nothing in our inquiry must be overlooked. One murder is quite enough.'

Later, when she was leaving the study after more questioning, the inspector said pleasantly, 'Oh, and I believe it is you we have to thank for the coffee? It was very good. The Château du Bois will miss you greatly when you go. You seem to have settled in very well – for a visitor.'

Sara found Steve sitting slumped in the drawing-room. 'Where's Jules?' she asked.

He barely opened his mouth. 'Gone to find Madame Darle.'

'Is there any coffee left?'

'It's cold.'

'I don't care.'

He looked up. 'Bad as that, was it?'

'That insufferable man! Treating me as if I was some love-sick girl trying to make an impression on the man of the house. He didn't believe a word I said – at least, that's the impression he gave me.'

'He probably starts on the premise that everyone is an inveterate liar and works his way down from there,' Steve said.

'How was I supposed to have shot my own tyre?' Sara demanded.

194

'You weren't. You were supposed to get rattled, and you obviously did. I bet there wasn't anything you didn't tell him after that.'

She gulped down some cold coffee. Then she looked at Steve more closely. 'Are you OK, Steve?' she asked softly, having noticed his pallor.

'Oh, sure. I'm fine.' His voice was laced with sarcasm. 'My aunt is found murdered and I feel fine.'

'I'm sorry,' she whispered.

He reached out and held her hand for a moment before speaking again. 'I'll never forget it as long as I live. I was there, you know – when they brought her in. I was down at the lake with a girl from the village.' He glanced up quickly. 'Everybody goes a bit mad on fête day. I don't even know her name! Anyway, we heard this commotion and went to see what was happening.

'One of the men fishing had caught something on the anchor – dragged out of the weed at the bottom of the lake. The others went to help him and . . . and . . .'

'Don't, Steve. Don't.'

'She had been there all the time, Sara!'

'I know.' Her heart went out to him. 'I

195

know.'

'She . . . she was unrecognisable!' Suddenly he jumped up and ran from the room, one hand over his mouth.

The night seemed to be going on for ever.

'He left the hospital too soon,' Jules said, after Steve had gone to bed.

Sara was past sleep. She nodded in agreement and shivered.

'Here, put this round you,' Jules said, taking off his jacket.

'No!' she answered sharply, then, relaxing, added her thanks softly.

He glanced at her, surprised. But Sara knew she would never be able to accept his friendship again – not the sort that had been slowly growing between them.

Not after what the inspector had hinted at so slyly. He had made her feel dirty and ashamed, inferring that she had tried to step into Helen's shoes. She had wanted to scream at him that she had not wanted to fall in love with Jules.

She wondered how much the inspector actually knew? Had he been having Jules watched? She remembered Steve telling her the police questioned Jules from time to time about Helen. How they were uneasy about her never contacting Michael. Had there been someone watching them both in Paris? She had felt closer to him there than anywhere; it had made her deliriously happy – and all the time Helen had been lying . . . She choked back the thought.

'Why don't you take yourself off to bed?' Jules said suddenly.

'Why don't you?' She clenched her fists. 'I'm sorry. I will.'

'I should like this diary you have – first.'

She had forgotten about it. Now she felt guilty for wondering if he did already know about it – and its contents. Why had the police questioned him twice?

'I should give it to the police,' she said stubbornly.

'I wish to see it first. I have that right.'

'Are you sure you haven't already seen it?' Why are you quizzing him? she asked herself. Hasn't he been through enough? But tiredness, confusion, and guilt were driving her on. Like a lemming heading for destruction.

'Of course I haven't seen it,' he snapped.

'Why did the police keep you in the study for so long?'

'Helen was my wife! I happened to know her intimately!'

197

'But you didn't know she went with men from the village?' The words were out before she could stop them.

He stared at Sara, a hard expression in his eyes. There was a long silence between them. She hated herself. She hated him. She wished she had never come to France – never heard of Jules Clare.

'So – what if I did know?' he said at last in a steely voice. The room spun round her. He began to walk towards her, his broad-shouldered figure growing taller with every step.

At that moment, a weird, unearthly sound shattered the funereal silence of the château. The sound of an animal in agony.

It was a man screaming!

Jules hurried from the room and Sara followed. People appeared from everywhere; running in the direction of the cellars. The inspector caught up with Jules.

It was icy-cold down there. Like a grey stone tomb.

Jules swung round and gripped Sara's arms. 'Don't look!' he cried. But it was too late. She had seen.

Pascal was kneeling on the floor. His arms, red and sweating in spite of the temperature, were outstretched as if imploring.

198

Fluid trickled from his eyes, his nose and his lips. Loud, hysterical sobs shook his hairy body.

Above him, Madame Darle dangled from a rope by her neck, like an old rag-doll.

Chapter Twenty-Three

SARA woke up the following morning with a raging headache. She stayed in the shower a long time, as though trying to wash away the horrible events of the past twenty-four hours. For the first time in many days there were clouds riding in the sky, but it was not cold. Sara wore a sleeveless navy dress. She wanted to show respect for Madame's memory, but the colour only seemed to enhance the vividness of her hair.

'The diary,' she said to Jules, when she found him in his study, and handed it over. He was gaunt and sad-looking. 'I'm so very sorry about Madame,' she added softly.

'She has been at the Château du Bois for as long as I can remember. None of us will ever forget her. She became my surrogate mother when my own mother died.'

'And Pascal? How is he?'

He shook his head. 'I doubt if he will ever get over this.'

'Why did she do it?' she asked.

'She could not bear the guilt any longer – but I can't believe—'

'What guilt?'

'She left a note saying she killed Helen,' he said dully.

Sara could not speak, only stare. The ringing of the telephone made her start.

Jules picked it up. 'Hello? Hello, Inspector,' he said in a flat voice. 'Yes, I will – what time did you say? Oh, and I have a document that will no doubt interest you. A diary has been found belonging to my wife. Yes, I will do that.'

'Why tell him about it now?' Sara asked after he replaced the receiver.

'What do you want me to do? Hide it?' He started to flick over the pages, his frown deepening. 'My God, I didn't expect to see these names.'

'But you have seen it before.'

'That is where you are wrong. I did not know this book existed until you told me about it.'

'But you said you knew—'

'I said I knew about Helen's promiscuity. A man does not have to have it written down for him to know when his wife is – how do you say? "Playing around." One lover – a hundred lovers; it's all the same. There are ways he can tell.'

Sara felt a sudden anxiety for him. He was about to present the police with a motive for Helen's murder. His motive.

'I – I don't see any point in complicating the issue now that Madame has confessed to the murder,' she told him nervously.

'Do you think anyone will believe she did it? Do you think I believe it? Or the police? No, she was not capable of—' He stalked to the door. 'Anyway, none of this concerns you – except perhaps to confirm a suspicion that was beginning to grow in your mind—'

'No, Jules!'

'Why not? All the evidence points to me. Madame could well have been trying to shield me.'

'I know you could never . . .' she began miserably, but Jules had already reached the door. He turned to her with a short, cynical laugh. 'You and Steve make a fine pair of sleuths.'

After he had gone, she pressed the palm of her hand against her forehead. 'Damn!'

she whispered. 'Damn, damn!'

When she saw Steve later he still looked very weary. 'Wouldn't you be better resting today, Steve?'

'I have just heard about Madame! It's the most awful – what's happening here, Sara? Tell me that. Who is going to be next?'

'She committed suicide, Steve.'

'You believe that, do you?' he asked grimly.

That afternoon, Sara set out walking to the village. The wind had started to blow strongly. She was glad. It was good to feel it whipping against her skin after the close, strained atmosphere in the château.

The village was almost deserted as she made her way to Pierre and Claudette's house. When she reached it she was surprised to see how many people were packed in there, including Henri and Arla. As soon as she entered the small, front room she could sense the shocked state among Pierre's murmuring friends.

They had obviously heard about Helen. Perhaps Madame, too? She was not sure. However, they welcomed her with a warmth she had not felt from them since first coming to the village.

'We have been waiting for Klaus for nearly an hour,' Pierre told her worriedly. 'I do not know what could have happened. He is always a very punctual man. I am sure he would have let us know if he was going to be late. I do hope he has not had an accident.'

'For goodness' sake, Pierre, don't burden Sara with our troubles,' Claudette protested. 'She must be very upset already after what has happened at the château. Poor Madame Clare.'

'Madame Clare deserved all she got!' a strident voice exclaimed.

Heads turned to look at Louise, normally a coarse-faced woman, but now with a particularly vicious expression about her. There was a strained silence. No one present had any love for Helen, but they would never have expected such an opinion openly, especially in front of a visitor from the château.

Pierre looked uncomfortable and spoke softly to Sara. 'Louise insisted on coming to the meeting. She says she is like family.' He shrugged. 'I suppose she is. She has been with us for many years – but I wish—' He shook his head solemnly.

'Why do we all pretend?' Louise asked

loudly. 'We did not like her. She made trouble.'

'Louise, dear – please don't speak ill of the dead,' Claudette said, frowning.

'The dead are better off than we are! At least they have had their fun.'

'Yes,' another woman said quietly. 'It is for Madame Darle we should be grieving.'

For a moment, Sara thought Louise was going to lash out with another bitter remark, but instead her face became contorted. She turned suddenly and rushed from the room, elbowing people aside as she did so.

'What is wrong with Louise?' Arla asked.

'She has been talking to Pascal on the phone,' Claudette said. 'It has upset her. You know how close they were. He is like a man demented.'

Sara stayed at the house as long as she could, but when Klaus still did not come, she decided she should go back to the château.

Jules had gone to see the police and Steve was not well. She had to help where she could. She was going to ignore the inspector's meaningful remark about her having settled in well for a visitor. He could think what he liked.

Pierre was full of apologies. 'As soon as I hear from Klaus I will contact you,' he said. 'We shall meet again very soon.'

'Oh, dear, and you are leaving Laffeine, are you not?' Claudette said to Sara.

'I may have to wait a little longer while the police carry out their inquiries on Madame Darle.' She noticed Henri look up quickly when she said this and then, as she left the house, she saw him limp after her.

'Can you hear the thunder, Henri? I think we are in for a storm,' she said pleasantly.

'Sara, I heard what you just said to Claudette. Forgive an old man for speaking his mind, but I strongly advise you not to remain in Laffeine a moment longer than you need to. Please – take notice of what I say.'

'Henri, didn't you once say I had my grandfather's spirit? Would he have run away?'

'It is not a question of running away . . .'

'Don't worry. My cases are already packed.'

'That is good. You are very wise.'

'But you've made me curious. I did not expect you . . .'

'Laffeine is like a place on the edge of a volcano. Once Klaus has told us all he

205

knows about the informer there will be a massive eruption here.'

'I wish I had never started all this in the first place,' Sara said wistfully. 'I should have just taken photos of grandfather's grave and left. I think I would have done, too, had it not been for the threats.'

'But you have brought us all together against the common enemy, do you not realise that? Now we will have our dignity and our pride again. As soon as our revenge is complete.'

'Oh, Henri – not you as well. Surely you know you can't go taking matters into your own hands? There are laws to . . .'

'I knew that would be your opinion,' he said, an edge of impatience in his voice. 'Pierre should never have told you.'

'Or invited me to the meeting? That is what you think, isn't it?'

'You are like the young ones in the village. None of you know about the reality of war.'

'A war that finished years ago,' she pointed out.

Sara saw the curtains move at one of the windows then Pierre's face disappearing. She frowned. Was Henri the spokesman for all of them? Why? What were they afraid of?

Then realisation dawned. They all thought she might be troubled by conscience and warn the police they were going to take the law into their own hands when they discovered who the traitor was. She felt a surge of anger. She might not approve, but she was not an informer.

'You have done your bit,' Henri was saying. 'Now go home.'

She turned on him sharply. 'Don't tell me what I can or cannot do, Henri!'

'He is our leader. You must do as he says,' a voice behind Sara said.

She turned to see Pierre standing quite near.

'Leader! What sort of game are you two playing?'

'No game,' Henri spoke severely. 'This is not one of Monsieur Clare's mystery stories we are trying to unravel. We act for all those who were betrayed. We act for the dead.'

The two elderly faces were unblinking, oblivious of the rain now falling.

Sara shivered and pulled up the hood of her anorak. 'Then let them rest in peace. When you find your traitor hand him over to . . .' She stopped. She could see it was no use. They were reliving a time that was only a page in a history book to her. United in a common purpose. And they were enjoying it.

She turned to leave them. Henri called, 'Don't forget. Everything you have heard is confidential.'

'And don't forget that I am a free agent. I can do and say what I like.'

'No! You are now part of us.'

Suddenly she realised it was true. The minute she had set foot in Laffeine and started making inquiries about her grandfather, she had become involved in their affairs. She was a part of them whether or not they were heading for disaster – and prison.

Whatever they decided to do, she must hold her tongue. This was no ordinary peacetime situation as far as they were concerned, they were acting out the rules of war, taking over where they had all left off, with Henri as their leader.

She was afraid of the old men of Laffeine.

She also felt concern for Louise, thinking of the expression on her face. A mixture of anger and misery, Sara thought, as she hurried back to the château, her head down against the beating storm. What was smouldering inside Louise? She and Pascal were a strange pair.

Sara wished she had taken one of the cars. Her summer shoes were no match for the uneven country lanes swimming with water. She remembered Steve insisting he was much better and saying he was going out for a walk. She hoped he had changed his mind.

She was halfway along the small road to the château when suddenly she heard a tremendous cracking noise behind her. She turned quickly, then ran on as fast as she could as one of the old trees on the edge of the field creaked ominously and fell across the road, spreading out gnarled, leafy branches like arms.

After that she raced the rest of the way, glancing worriedly at the other trees that lined her path. Once inside the château, she banged the door behind her and leaned against it, breathless and drenched through her coat.

'Jacqueline,' she gasped, as the maid appeared. 'One of the trees is down and it's completely blocking the road to the château. Where is Monsieur Clare?'

'He is at the police station, Mademoiselle.'

'Still there?'

The two women exchanged anxious glances.

'Then you had better telephone,' Sara began.

'I cannot telephone anyone. It is out of order again,' Jacqueline said.

Sara sighed. 'It's the storm. It can't be helped. You took care of Michael as we arranged?'

'Yes – but Monsieur Steve said he would take him for a walk.'

'Oh, no! Steve is not well.'

'He looked a little better,' Jacqueline assured her. 'And they have their boots on . . . they will shelter. Come, M'moiselle, you must get out of those wet clothes.' She was helping Sara off with her anorak when a brilliant flash of lightning lit up the wide hall, illuminating the tapestries, and bringing the family portraits to life.

'I do not like—' Jacqueline stopped what she was saying and her eyes widened.

Sara followed her gaze towards the stairs. A white-robed figure was staggering down towards them.

'Help me! Help me!' Crystal cried, then she collapsed.

Chapter Twenty-Four

SARA leaned over the bed and spoke gently. 'Try to relax, Crystal.'

'Where am I?' Crystal sobbed.

'We brought you to my room. I thought you would be more comfortable here.'

'But where is the doctor?' Crystal lifted herself on her elbows, then fell back on the pillow with a groan.

Sara swallowed. When she spoke, she sounded more calm than she felt. 'One of the maids has gone to fetch him.'

'I need him now! Why do you not telephone?' She screwed up her face and started moaning, drawing up her knees to her stomach.

'He will be here shortly. You will be all right, I promise.' Sara felt beads of perspiration on her own body, too.

'How do you know?' Crystal snapped. 'Have you ever had a baby?'

Sara went to look for Jacqueline. 'Are the jugs of hot water ready?' Then a scream from Crystal took her quickly back to the bedroom.

'I can't bear it! I'm dying!' she shouted.

Sara wiped the girl's forehead after the contraction passed. 'Do you want to push?'

she asked her.

'I don't want to do anything. And I don't want this baby!'

'Well, you are having it! So the sooner you accept that and get on with it the better.'

Crystal glared. Then her lips quivered. 'It hurts, Sara.'

Sara held her hand. 'I'll bet it does,' she murmured. 'But I would change places with you if I could have a child by the man I love.'

'I love my man – but he doesn't love me.' Crystal was suddenly more calm than Sara had seen her. She sat quietly while the girl talked. 'When I first knew I was pregnant, I was really scared in case Madame Clare came back and found out. She would have sacked me on the spot. And jobs like this are hard to find.' She began to sweat. 'Why have you got a handkerchief round your mouth?'

'You don't want my germs breathed over your baby, do you?'

'You are kind to me. No one has been kind to me for a long time. Except Monsieur.'

'You like him, don't you?'

'I knew he would not sack me. I said he

wouldn't. But she was different.'

'And the baby's father? What did he say?'

'He said I needn't worry.' She gave a throaty gasp and closed her eyes. 'He said . . . she would never come back to Laffeine again . . . that . . . he had . . . seen to it . . .'

'Who is the baby's father, Crystal?' Sara asked in a hoarse voice.

'If I tell you – you must promise to tell no one . . . or he will kill us both. The baby! The baby! Don't leave me!'

'I won't leave you.'

Crystal was squeezing Sara's hand so tightly it made her wince.

'Promise you won't tell?' Crystal panted. She spluttered the name. Then she lifted her head and gave a piercing scream . . .

.

'It's a little girl, Crystal,' Sara whispered some time later, her heart at last slowing down. With trembling hands, she laid the baby gently in Crystal's arms.

The two women gazed at the child.

'She has eyes like my mother,' Crystal said softly.

'She is just beautiful! Beautiful!' Sara whispered.

'Yes.'

Then they looked at one another with tears brimming. They both laughed out loud.

Crystal blinked hard. 'I shall call her Sara. Tell the others. I want them all to see my baby.'

There was a noise in the passage outside.

'That must be Jacqueline,' Sara said. She went to open the door in time to glimpse someone disappearing round the corner, then she heard the sound of running feet. On the floor was a man's handkerchief.

Someone had been listening at the door. He must have heard Crystal tell her the name of the murderer. Sara closed the door with trembling hands. Now her life was in grave danger.

'Who was it?' Crystal asked.

'No one. Probably one of the cats, I expect.'

'He is here, Mademoiselle. The doctor is here,' Jacqueline shouted.

Crystal glanced anxiously at Sara. 'Remember. You promised never to tell.'

While the doctor was with Crystal, Sara went to the kitchen to organise some tea. She had never felt so tired in her life. She dropped on to a chair, drained of all energy. Then she saw Jacqueline dabbing her eyes.

'Whatever's wrong, Jacqueline?'

'It is Monsieur Clare. When Sophie came back with the doctor, she told me the police have arrested him. For Madame Clare's murder.'

Chapter Twenty-Five

EVERYTHING in Sara's head was spinning. How could the police be so stupid? She flattened her hand against the scrubbed wooden table and pushed herself to her feet. Her knees were shaking.

'I have to go and see Crystal straight away,' she said.

'Oh, not now, M'moiselle,' Jacqueline protested. 'The doctor is with her. Please – sit down and rest.' The maid was twisting her handkerchief into tight knots.

Then her French became difficult for Sara to understand because she started gabbling on about having neither master nor mistress in the château and what was going to happen to all of them who worked there.

'Monsieur Jules did not do it! Don't you understand?' Sara asked in exasperation.

She had a sudden urge to grab hold of the maid and shake her. Then she realised that shaking and shouting would only be ways of working out her own guilt. But why should she feel guilty? Why did there lurk in the deepest recesses of her mind a feeling that everything that had happened was somehow linked with her?

She told herself she might have felt easier if, all the time she was falling in love with Jules, Helen had been living it up with one of her lovers instead of rotting in the silt of a murky lake.

'I should never have come here,' she said aloud.

'Of course you should!' a warm, sensible voice assured her.

Sara looked round in astonishment and saw Mary Betts bustling into the kitchen.

'Mary! What are you . . .?'

'I had to come back – after what I read in the newspapers. Such terrible things have been happening here. I can't believe it. And you – you look completely exhausted. Jacqueline, stop dithering about and bring us some scones and tea.'

'But—'

'Croissants, then – anything you like!'

Sara was glad to let Mary take over. It felt

good to have her back.

A moment later the doctor followed her into the room, smiling at Sara.

'You did a very good job up there, my dear. Mother and daughter are doing very well.'

'It's something I wouldn't like to have done on my own,' Mary said ruefully. 'Especially with that one. She's temperamental even on her best days.'

The doctor grinned. 'Well, she's feeling very pleased with herself now and is delighted to have a daughter. I'll be sending a nurse along as soon as the road is cleared.'

'How did you get here?' Sara asked.

'I had to leave the car and do a bit of scrambling through the fields, but I managed it all right. Now' – he looked squarely at Sara – 'how are you feeling? Exhausted? Would you like me to give you something?'

'No, I'm fine, really.' She escorted him to the door, then asked quietly, 'Doctor is – is it true that Monsieur Clare has been arrested?'

'That is what everyone is saying.' He looked at her with sharp, brown eyes. 'Do not worry, my child.'

She glanced around her quickly. 'Doctor

– I think the police should send somebody up here.'

'You do?' He raised an eyebrow. 'I would say everything is going very smoothly now.'

'It's nothing to do with the baby.' She felt a deep frustration. If only she could tell him what Crystal had confided in her. 'It's just that I think we could be in some danger.'

He patted her hand. 'You kept your head when it was vitally important, and for that I congratulate you – but perhaps now a little reaction should be expected, no?'

'No!'

'Very well, I will call and tell Jacques of your worries.'

'Jacques?'

'The policeman in Laffeine. He will make sure you rest easy in your beds.'

'Thank you.'

'Try to get some rest. You are tired. Overwrought. It is understandable.'

You don't understand, she wanted to shout, but knew it would take too long to explain to the doctor.

After he had gone, she raced up the stairs and tapped on Crystal's door. When she entered the room, Sara was astonished at the change in her. She was sitting bolt upright in bed, wearing a revealing silky nightdress and holding up a mirror so that she could smooth orange lipstick liberally across her mouth.

'Can I speak to you, Crystal?' she asked, trying to sound calm. The other two maids, bending over the cradle at the side of the bed, scuttled out.

'You look radiant,' Sara added.

'The doctor said she was the most perfect of babies he had seen. I said to him—'

'Crystal,' Sara broke in, sitting down on the edge of the bed, 'there is something we have to talk about.'

'And I said to the doctor, "I was a beautiful baby myself; my mother"—'

'The police have arrested Monsieur Jules for his wife's murder.'

Crystal did not speak. The hand holding the mirror slowly dropped to rest on the duvet. Then she seemed to recover and she shrugged. 'Pah – they will not keep him. He will be released. Do not worry.'

'Crystal,' Sara said, her voice rising. 'Don't you understand? You will have to tell the police what you told me.'

'What do you mean? What I told you?' Crystal looked at Sara coldly.

'You know what I mean.'

'I was in such terrible pain, I do not

remember what I said,' the maid said petulantly.

'You remember very well. Oh Crystal – we have to help Jules. Look, are you scared to tell what you know? Are you afraid of what the baby's father might do to you? Please – don't be frightened. The police will arrest him and he will be taken away for ever.'

When she saw the expression that flooded Crystal's face, Sara knew she had said the wrong thing. The splitting pain of childbirth might have caused her to scream out what she knew, but already that pain was fading in her memory, and in spite of knowing her lover did not return her affection, she did not want him taken from her.

We women are fools, Sara thought. When we fall in love, there is no sense in us. We are lifted from reality on the swell of a wave and carried off to paradise. At least, that's what we think it is, but – whatever comes after, there is a part of us that stays committed to that man.

Now Crystal glared at her. 'You promised! If you told it would be sinful – like the priest telling about someone's confession.'

'But you can't let the wrong man be

accused.'

'I must protect my man as you would protect yours. And if you do say anything, I shall say you are making lies!'

'I thought you adored Jules and had reason to be grateful to him? You know you will never lack for a home – you and the baby, not while he is master here.'

Sara knew she should not have used that line of reasoning. She was even more sorry when the maid looked up, tears brimming in her eyes.

'You must understand. I thought I was going to die. I would never have—' suddenly, Crystal's expression tightened. 'I do not remember anything I said.' She leaned over the baby and stroked her cheek.

Had it not been for the circumstances, Sara knew the scene in front of her would have been perfect, almost religious. She knew, too, that she could never betray Crystal's confidences.

She stood up to leave. At the door, she turned and spoke softly. 'When I first came here I heard someone crying in one of the rooms.'

'So?'

'It came from your room, didn't it?'

'A lovers' quarrel, that was all.'

221

'He hit you, didn't he?' Sara persisted.

'I told you – a lovers' tiff.'

Sara remembered how Jacqueline looked as if she had heard the crying too, but had taken no notice. Was it because she was so used to hearing such quarrels?

Afterwards, Sara found Mary in Michael's room. 'I missed the château, Sara, and I missed Michael very much, even if he is a scamp,' Mary told her. She fingered a teddy-bear and added thoughtfully, 'I cannot bear to think that two women died here through such tragic circumstances.'

'I cannot imagine why Madame Darle should leave a note saying she killed Helen. So many lies . . .' Sara began.

'What lies? She had a reason like everyone else. There was no love lost between them – she loathed the way Helen cheated on her husband.'

'Did Madame Darle ever try to tell Jules what was going on?'

'Good heavens, no! And I know why. Helen once mentioned that she had Madame Darle just where she wanted her. Whatever it was, Madame Darle took Helen's secret to the grave with her.'

'There is no way she could have killed

Helen! Crystal . . .' Sara stopped at once, biting her lip.

Mary glanced at her curiously. 'Oh, my dear. I hope Crystal hasn't been spreading her stories again. She has a fertile imagination, that one. And she loves to be the centre of attention. Perhaps now she has a baby to think about she'll come down to earth a bit.'

'But you don't understand. I know she was telling the truth. And I shall never believe Madame Darle – or Jules – killed Helen, even if some folk do say he was having an affair with his secretary and . . .'

'That is absolute rubbish!' Mary exclaimed vehemently. 'Matilde has a husband and toddler at home. Oh, she may be flirtatious, but then – look at her; it is in her nature. I know there were some raised eyebrows when she started working late, but you see, it is more convenient for her then. She looks after her child during the day and her husband is there in the evening. Jules did not care when she did his typing. It was all the same to him.'

Sara felt her heart lighten. It was ridiculous, she told herself, but she could not help it.

'Jules would not be interested in any

woman, not after Helen,' Mary continued. 'He was crazy about her when they married, but she had her own set of rules on fidelity. Anyway, who has been filling your head with such tales? Steve?'

'I – I don't remember.'

'He's a strange one. He's like Crystal. What he doesn't know he makes up.'

'But he does seem to have insight of some sort.'

'He's more astute than most, and more intelligent,' Mary said firmly. 'And that goes a long way. But as for insight . . .' She frowned. 'He and Michael should be home by now.'

'He shouldn't be out in this rain with the boy.' Sara went on to tell Mary about Steve's illness and all that had happened. 'He is convinced someone tried to poison him.'

'That is ridiculous. Steve has no enemies.'

'He has since he started probing to find out what happened to Helen. I mean, everyone thought she had run away of her own accord. A murderer wouldn't want the whole thing opened up, and Steve finding her diary could mean questions by the police.'

'I shall be glad when we are all back to

normal again,' Mary said, sighing.

'Do you think we ever will be?'

'Oh, yes. Life has to go on.'

Mary was always so practical, so sensible, Sara thought. Her solid, down-to-earth attitude could make one look at events in a different perspective. She was probably right, and Crystal did have flights of fancy. Her story could be a pack of lies designed to attract attention. And perhaps Steve did have a knack of guessing what had or was about to happen.

Sara had almost convinced herself that most things could be put down to imagination, but as she left Mary and walked alone along the narrow passages of the château, she found herself stepping out quickly and her heart was beating faster.

The sound of the baby crying nearly made her jump out of her skin. She hurried to Crystal's room.

Crystal was standing by the window, the baby in her arms.

'Crystal! What are you doing out of bed?'

'I heard noises,' the maid cried. 'Outside my door. I was afraid.'

'Come on, let me take her, and you pop back into bed. It was only the sound of my footsteps you heard.'

'No! I heard a man cough. I called out, but nobody answered.' Her eyes were wide. 'He is out there! I know he is. Why did he not answer me?'

'I didn't see anyone. Please – get back into bed.'

Crystal was shaking. She handed Sara the baby. 'I grabbed her quickly. I was going to hide. Did I hurt her? Oh, see how she cries.'

'She's got a good pair of lungs on her; that's all to the good. I expect she's hungry.'

Crystal climbed into bed and stared miserably at Sara. 'I have been thinking about what you said. He did hit me. Many times. Suppose . . . suppose he hits my baby?'

She was talking in a slightly breathless way now. 'I have been frightened thinking about it. M'moiselle – he is a crazy man, but I don't want him arrested. But neither can I let him touch my baby.' She covered her face with her hands.

After a long time, she spoke again.

'If you get Jacques here, I will tell him what I know.'

The words were no sooner out of her mouth than the bedroom door was smashed open and Pascal's big, hairy body filled the opening like a great bear. His eyes were

226

burning bright. His hair and his clothes were soaking.

Then, to their horror, he lurched forward towards Sara and the baby.

Instinctively, her arms tightened round the tiny bundle. They were the only parts of her body that were not paralysed. Nothing else would move. She tried to scream but even her voice was gone.

He stopped in front of her and his powerful hand pulled the shawl back from the baby's face. He leered. Then he looked round at Crystal who was sitting up stiffly, like a statue, her face ashen.

'I shall come back for him,' he growled. 'I am going to be rich – and he will be rich.'

'Oh, God, what have you done, Pascal?' Crystal whispered.

The baby started to cry again. Pascal's lips were stretched into a grotesque smile. 'He cries good, my son.'

'But—' Crystal began.

'Yes, he does,' Sara interrupted before she could say any more. She did not want Crystal to upset him in any way. It could be the smallest thing that would push the man over the edge into complete and utter madness; even knowing his child was a girl.

She did not need to be a doctor to see that

he was mentally disturbed.

'He's very beautiful,' Sara continued, trying to control the tremor in her voice. 'You should be very proud of him.' She walked slowly and casually to the cradle and laid the baby down, covering her over.

'He hurt you, eh?' Pascal said to Crystal, as if the thought gave him pleasure. 'Made you scream?'

'You – you were listening!' Crystal said, eyes wide open in fear.

Pascal leaned over the cradle and gazed at the baby. 'I will come for you. You shall have everything.'

He looked hard at Sara. In that one moment, he appeared sane to her. 'You tell Monsieur he will be hearing from me! It will cost him dearly to get his son back.' He paused for a moment. 'Everything will be different. Now it will be my son who has the wealth,' he added with satisfaction.

Sara was icy cold down her spine. 'Michael – what have you done with Michael?' she asked hoarsely. 'And Steve?'

He waggled his finger from side to side mischievously. 'I will only tell Monsieur – when he has the money.' He stumbled to the door and caught hold of the handle. Then he seemed to change his mind and looked back at the cradle. 'I think it will be better if I take him now. You are a pig, Crystal. You will hide him.'

To Sara's astonishment, Crystal did not cry out as he rolled across the bedroom towards the baby. Instead, she stretched out her arm and caught Pascal's sleeve.

'I can keep him safe for you, Pascal; feed him, make him strong. You get the money first. Yes – he will be very rich. But you get the money first.' She was talking in a high-pitched, rapid tone, and her other hand was gripping the side of the cradle tightly.

Both women held their breath.

Then, at last, Pascal muttered, 'I want him strong.'

'He will be! I promise you,' Crystal said.

Sara could hardly breathe for relief. The next second, Pascal came up behind her and twisted her arm up against her back.

'You tell him,' he snarled viciously, 'if he wants to see the boy alive, not to tell the police. I will contact him. Understand?' He swung her round to face him.

She could see his bad teeth. She nodded, shaking.

He pulled her even closer.

Every fibre of her being urged her to fight him the ways she had been taught. But she dare not take the risk. Not with the baby in the room. She had to keep him sweet. So when he suddenly began to squeeze her she remained still and closed her eyes. He threw her to one side and began to march to the door. Then he turned. 'You can bring the money, Sara,' he said, leering at her.

After he had gone, Sara rushed to lock the door.

'He's crazy! No, mad!' Crystal yelled. 'For God's sake, don't leave me alone here.'

'Don't go to pieces now, Crystal – you've been so brave. I had no idea you could be so brave.' Sara spoke reassuringly.

Crystal blinked and said more calmly, 'It must have been his mother hanging herself. He only ever loved her – and—'

'Who?'

'Someone in the village. I heard talk.' She began to panic again. 'He'll be back. For my baby!'

'Listen – I'll get Mary. She'll stay with you.'

'Where are you going?'

'To the police. I have to! Michael's life depends on it.'

Chapter Twenty-Six

SHE ran in the rain until she was out of breath. She had reached the point where the road forked when she heard the sound of a car.

'Can I give you a lift?' a fresh-faced man asked, pulling up beside her.

'Please!' she gasped. 'I must get to the village quickly.'

In the car, he told her in a heavy accent that he was Pierre's friend, Klaus, and that he had been delayed by floods in one of the valleys.

After Sara had spilled out her story to Jacques, and he had immediately telephoned his inspector at the station where Jules was held in custody, Klaus insisted on taking her back to the château. When they reached the fallen tree, there was a tractor in the road dragging it to one side with a massive chain.

As Klaus drove through, Sara saw two hefty men clambering down with chainsaws.

She shuddered.

'Are you cold?'

She shook her head. 'I was just reminded of Pascal. I hope I did the right thing telling the police.'

'It was the only thing you could do. They are the experts when it comes to cases of kidnapping. Only they are equipped to deal with a maniac like Pascal.'

'You know him?'

'I once came to the château. It . . . it was before I knew Helen was married. Her husband was away at the time.' He added softly, 'It was the only time I came.'

His confession didn't mean anything to Sara. All she could think about was Michael – and the monster, Pascal. Suppose he had been skulking around watching her movements? Perhaps even now he knew where she had been? She felt sick at the thought of having precipitated Michael's death if it was so.

'I can't understand how Crystal ever came to love him!' she exclaimed. 'He really is psychotic.'

'Madness is not always apparent at the start. You only have to remember Hitler. Yet there was a woman at his side when he died, though I would very much doubt he was capable of a normal, loving relationship. His crimes against humanity will never be forgotten.'

Their eyes met. 'I know,' he added. 'My father fought for his country, but what he saw sickened him and haunted him until the day he died.'

Klaus remained at the château until two policemen came to protect the women, then he went on to the village to see Pierre.

There was no sign of Pascal, but Sara knew they would be hearing from him. She was told that everything was in hand and there was nothing more she could do. It was eerie somehow that the media was maintaining an absolute silence on the kidnapping. They had obviously had their instructions.

Mary and Sara shared the same thoughts as they sat together in the drawing-room.

'Why haven't they found him?' Mary demanded, showing uncharacteristic impatience.

'I suppose they have to move slowly. Pascal must not find out the police are involved.'

Mary thumped at a cushion. 'I know. I just can't stand the waiting. I only thank God Steve is with the wee boy. To be out there alone with Pascal . . . it's terrible to think about.'

'Listen! What was that?'

'I didn't hear anything.'

'I thought I heard something,' Sara said.

'I'll just go and make sure Crystal is all right.'

Mother and baby were fast asleep. There was a faint, sweet smell of clean laundered sheets and baby talc.

Sara stared through the window to the distant woods. Were Michael and Steve out there somewhere? Under the dripping trees, shivering and hungry? Was Crystal right, that his mother's death had been the trigger that shot into Pascal's already unquiet mind? Were any of them ever going to feel safe again?

She had reached the hall again when she heard the same noise – a dull thud from outside. She went to open the main door.

Steve slithered in and fell, wet and bleeding, at her feet.

'What did the doctor say?' Mary asked after Steve had been examined.

Words stuck in Sara's throat. At last she managed to speak. 'All he remembers is being hit on the head. When he came round he was lying in a ditch full of water. By some miracle his head was jammed against a stone just above water level.'

'And Michael had gone?'

Sara nodded. 'The two of them had been

sheltering from the rain, but when there was no sign of it stopping they decided to make a run for home. Steve stopped for a minute to tie the lace of his boot and called Michael to wait for him. That was the last thing he remembers. He's chilled to the bone but the doctor says he'll be all right.'

For a long time the women were silent.

At last, Sara whispered, 'I'm going to look for Michael.'

'Me, too.'

'No, if we both disappear from the château the police will suspect something's up. You stay and cover for me. Besides, as far as Pascal is concerned, only Crystal and me know about him. If I meet him I'll talk my way out of it somehow.'

'It's dangerous, Sara!'

'You are willing to go.'

'I'm Michael's nanny.'

'Then he'll need you if – when – he comes home.'

'Oh, be careful. Be careful.'

Sara tried to convince herself Pascal had not had enough time to get Michael out of the area. That there was a chance she might find the little boy. She trod gently under the canopy of branches in the wood, the smell of damp earth filling her nostrils. Whatever happened, she could no longer sit and wait. She had not gone far when she heard voices nearby and froze against a tree.

'I reckon he'll have got that little lad right out of the district by now. Damn lot of good this is. He'd be a fool to stay around here.'

'Well, he's mad, isn't he? And a pervert with it, by all accounts . . .'

The voices of the policemen faded into the thicket beyond Sara. She caught her breath. She ought to have known men would be out searching. She could be doing more harm than good.

She was about to turn back when she saw one of Jules' boats rocking on the water at the edge of the lake. She crept stealthily towards the jetty. It had stopped raining, but the ground was a carpet of thick mud. Her feet slipped and squelched.

She had almost reached the moored boat when suddenly a hand was clapped over her mouth. She could scarcely breathe, let alone utter a sound.

'Bitch! You told the police!' Pascal hissed into her ear. 'Well – you know what that means. The boy will die. And so will you. But first . . .'

She could scarcely believe what he started to do next. She clawed and fought like a

236

wild cat within the iron restraint of his thick arms. In a nightmarish replay, she remembered Jules telling her: 'Your little knowledge of the martial arts would not be sufficient to protect you from what many men have first and foremost on their minds.'

He had spoken the truth. She kicked and scratched, and brought up her knee – all in vain. He threw her to the ground like a bundle of rags.

'Lie still or you are dead!' he threatened. 'I warned you to get out of Laffeine, but you took no notice of my note. Now you shall see . . .'

The cry that escaped from her throat was like a sob. In that instant, she felt the enormous weight lifted from her. She saw Jules grappling with him. The two men fell into the mud and rolled over and over in a frenzy of legs and arms.

Jules smashed his fist into Pascal's mouth. Pascal rose to his feet like a great, lumbering monster, red froth on his lips. He grabbed a fallen branch and raised it above his head.

Jules dodged to the side as it crashed down and threw himself at Pascal's legs.

'Hold him, Monsieur!' someone cried.

Pascal looked round startled and saw the line of police running towards him. With a desperate effort he heaved himself away from Jules, dived into the lake with a great splash, and began to swim fast and furiously.

'Don't shoot!' someone shouted.

Then Sara saw Pascal disappear under the murky water. She was not sure if he was trying to mask the direction in which he was swimming – or whether something had happened to him.

She felt a coat draped round her shoulders and one of the policemen saying gently, 'Are you all right, M'moiselle?'

She nodded miserably and drew the coat tightly round her.

Several of the men went out on to the lake to look for Pascal and his body, like Helen's, was dragged up from the weeds.

Chapter Twenty-Seven

JULES and Sara sat in silence in front of a freshly-lit log fire. At last he said quietly, 'I saw you trying to fight him off. You were very brave.'

'I shudder to think what might have happened if you had not appeared when you did. I owe you so much.'

'And I am grateful you went looking for Michael – but oh, Sara, it was foolish in the circumstances.'

'I know,' she agreed miserably.

He stood up and began to pace the room. 'For God's sake! Wouldn't you think they would have found some trace of him by now?'

'Are they still searching the woods?'

'I hope so. I hope they flatten every blade of grass and every damn precious plant—'

'Is that why you haven't wanted us to stray from the paths? Rare plants?'

'Yes, it was my mother's major interest. I tried to preserve them as she had done.' He closed his eyes as if very tired. 'Priorities! What the hell does it matter now? All I want is for Mike to be safe.'

'Oh, I know he will be!' she exclaimed. She wanted to convince herself as much as him. When he had turned up in the woods she had wanted to cry with joy, especially after she heard the police had released him.

He nodded solemnly. 'Yes.' Then his eyes searched her face. 'Thank God we weren't too late for you,' he whispered.

She held her whole body tense, just as she had done in the woods, to stop herself from falling into his arms. The strain of being in the same room as him was increasing by the minute, and she was glad when Jacqueline came in to say she was wanted on the phone.

'Sara, I had to ring you,' Pierre said urgently. 'It is finished. We cannot carry on.'

'Pierre, what's the matter? What has happened? Did Klaus come to see you?'

'Yes,' he said slowly. 'And he told us who the traitor was. Now we know – we cannot – there has been too much suffering. At one time it was decided among us that should the traitor be dead already, we would deal with any living members of the family left behind. This we now find ourselves unable to do. You see – we have not only heard from Klaus, but from—' She heard him draw in a sobbing breath. 'Enough is enough. It is finished!'

'Pierre – who?'

'Expect a visitor,' he said briefly, and put down the phone.

She went slowly back to Jules. 'It was Pierre. He is completely distraught. He knows who betrayed them in the war.

'Oh.' His voice was flat.

She stared at him. 'You know, don't you?'

'I do not know, but I have—'

The bell outside clanged. They both rushed towards the door as the maid opened it. Sara stifled a gasp.

Big, burly Louise stood with tears streaming down her face. She held Michael by the hand. He ran forward with a cry and threw his small body at Jules.

The next day, Sara drove away from Laffeine the way she had come. But instead of the air of excitement and anticipation she had felt on entering Burgundy, now there was only a dull ache inside her and the knowledge she had turned a village upside down.

As long as she lived she would remember Louise sitting beside the fire, clutching a cup of coffee in her trembling hands. Brave Louise, who had killed a snake with her bare hands, now gazing pitifully at Jules with swollen, red-rimmed eyes, an unmistakable plea for understanding. Her words were etched on Sara's mind.

'I loved Pascal, Monsieur. And he loved

me. His mother realised, and told him what had happened. At the beginning of the war Pascal's father was sent to a concentration camp. Madame Darle was very much in love with him. The Gestapo found her an easy target for blackmail – a young, impressionable girl.

'She believed them when they said it would go well for her husband if she co-operated with them. Her weakness caused the death of the many men she betrayed. Then – then she became pregnant by a German officer. She left the village and went to her sister's. When she returned to Laffeine she left me – the baby – behind.'

Louise's voice was bitter. 'No one here knew about me. Her sister kept me until the war was over. When she died, my uncle brought me to Laffeine. Even then my – "mother" refused to take me in – her bastard by a German.

'She persuaded an old couple to look after her poor, motherless "niece." As soon as I was old enough I went to work for Pierre, the butcher, and his wife. They showed me the first real kindness I had ever known in my life. They treated me like a daughter.'

'And they never knew you were Madame Darle's child?'

Louise shook her head. 'Not until today.' The tears came again. She bit her lip. 'I have done everything to protect Pascal, Monsieur. But not this! I cannot do this!'

She rubbed her broad hands down her cheeks to wipe the tears away, but still they flowed. 'He – he brought Michael to me. He told me I was to hide him until he came for him. That I was to tell no one or he would be put into prison. Oh, Monsieur! I could not do it. I could not let him hurt a child!'

'I know.' Jules took her hands gently in his. 'I know you couldn't, Louise. Tell me what else you have done to help him.'

Louise nodded towards Sara. 'When she started sniffing around – opening up the case of the British soldier, Pascal was terrified our mother would be discovered for the traitor she was. It had all been forgotten for years! I knew he would do something dreadful. I wanted to warn her off – that was all.'

'You shot at me in the churchyard?' Sara asked in amazement.

'I meant to miss you, and I did. But still you stayed!'

'And the other attempts on my life – these were all arranged by Pascal?'

'You must understand – Pascal was sick.

He adored his mother. He would have died to keep her secret hidden. And I – I was too ashamed to confide in anyone. It was my secret, too.'

'Have you told Pierre all this?' Jules asked.

She nodded. 'The whole village was at boiling point. But when I told them my story they – they did nothing. They said . . .' She had difficulty getting out the words. 'They said I had suffered greatly and that – they loved me.' She whispered the last three words again. 'They loved me.'

When she had recovered, Jules asked her softly, 'And it was Pascal who tampered with Steve's food?'

'He was learning too much about your wife, Monsieur.'

'But what does Helen have to do with Madame Darle?'

'She was the only person who knew about Madame Darle. The only person Klaus ever told – until now. He must have let it slip in an unguarded moment. He is not the sort of person who makes mischief.'

'Of course – one of her lovers,' Jules said caustically.

'And so she was able to blackmail Madame Darle. My mother kept all her

244

secrets from you Monsieur – when she left the château at night, who she met . . .'

'Oh, my God!' Jules buried his head in his hands for a few moments. 'And so Pascal killed Helen to stop her from opening her mouth to anyone else in the village. And he must have forced her to write her signature on the note, saying she was leaving me. Did he write his mother's letter as well, confessing she had killed Helen?' Jules demanded.

'Oh, no. When the body was found, it must have been too much for her. She would have suspected Pascal. She had to protect him as he had protected her.' Louise slowly lifted her hands, almost in a praying gesture. 'Oh, Monsieur, I am so very, very sorry.'

'Louise, you brought back my son. That is everything I want,' Jules told her sincerely.

Everything I want, Sara repeated to herself now, as she glanced in the driving mirror, seeing only blurred images. She recalled Jules shaking hands with her so formally when she left. How ironic that the sun should begin to shine now!

She had resolved to throw herself into hard work the moment she arrived home.

245

But first, she had to see Matthew, and explain as gently as she was able to that she could not marry him. He was the sort of person who would accept this philosophically. He was that type of man – and too nice, she told herself, for her to marry out of loneliness. That was not fair.

The only cheerful thought in her head was that Steve had said he would keep in touch. He and Jules had had some sort of reconciliation, and now Steve was off to pick grapes.

Sara had joked that the outdoor life would put the roses back into his cheeks, and was preferable to him brooding over the runes half the night.

'Oh, but I'm taking those with me,' he had said. 'They stretch the mind.' Her mind would be stretched too. She knew that one day next summer, when she stood in a sunny, dusty classroom, she would reach out to where a little boy might be playing in a rambling old château. Or where a tall, lean figure was striding out across the woods.

She frowned. Someone was waving to her from a lay-by ahead. She did not intend to stop this time for hitch-hikers. Then she identified the Porsche and the man standing there.

'Jules! What . . .?'

He strolled over to her car and folded his arms. 'I was thinking. You haven't had a proper holiday yet. You shall have one now.'

'But I have to get back,' Sara protested feebly.

He ignored her, and, to her astonishment, started to remove her luggage.

She jumped out of the car. 'Jules, what do you . . .'

He turned and grasped her arms. She stared up into his deep blue eyes. She had never seen such tenderness in them.

'How can I let you go, Sara? How can I?' He took her in his arms and kissed her.

'I have a villa in the south. Come with me,' he murmured.

She glanced behind her at her car, at the cases ready to be transferred to his car.

'No more looking back, Sara,' he whispered. 'Especially after we are married.'

She wanted to tell him he was far too sure of himself, but as he ran his fingers through her hair, there was no time for talking. And as she sat beside him in the Porsche, she experienced a delirious happiness. A happiness that was to endure.

The publishers hope that this book has given you enjoyable reading. Large Print Books are especially designed to be as easy to see and hold as possible. If you wish a complete list of our books, please ask at your local library or write directly to: Dales Large Print, Long Preston, North Yorkshire, BD23 4ND England.